DRIVE me CRAZY

Todd Strasser

ALADDIN PAPERBACKS

To Sheila Strasser,
who taught me to keep trying

First Aladdin Paperbacks edition October 1999

Text copyright © 1996 by Todd Strasser
Cover art and interior stills copyright © 1999 Twentieth Century Fox Film Corporation

Aladdin Paperbacks
An imprint of Simon & Schuster
Children's Publishing Division
1230 Avenue of the Americas, New York, NY 10020

Designed by Heather Wood
The text for this book was set in Janson.
Printed and bound in the United States of America.
10   9   8   7   6   5   4   3   2   1

The Library of Congress has cataloged a previous edition as follows:
Strasser, Todd. How I created my perfect prom date / Todd Strasser. — 1st ed.   p. cm.
Summary: When Brad asks someone else to the senior prom, Nicole resorts to a desperate measure—she decides to make her next-door neighbor over into a dream date.
[1. Proms—Fiction. 2. High schools—Fiction. 3. Schools—Fiction. 4. Interpersonal relations—Fiction.]
I. Title.   PZ7.S899Gi 1996
[Fic]—dc20   96-10569
ISBN 0-689-83115-3 (pbk.)

DRIVE me CRAZY

NICOLE

The thing I love the most about parties is being invited. Going is a different story. But that invitation makes me feel included. It tells me that I'm liked enough, or respected enough (or maybe even feared enough!), that they want me to be there.

Yes, I admit it, I like being the *P* word.

Oh, go ahead and call me superficial. But don't forget that this is high school. Of course there are more important things than being invited to parties, buying clothes, and dating the best-looking boys.

Deep inside we all know it's silly and immature and *blah, blah, blah* to care who asks who to the prom. But what else am I supposed to do? I can't vote, my mother won't let me have a job, and homework takes about a nanosecond.

The phone's ringing for the hundredth time tonight. It's probably Alicia, but maybe, just maybe, it's Brad Selden calling to ask me to the prom. I'm going to answer it in a second, but first I want to give you my word on something. Don't laugh. This is totally sincere. I, Nicole Maris, swear that I'm going to get serious about life. Really. I'm going to find a cause or disease or something to devote myself to. Something that will help the environment or my fellow man or whatever.

But first Brad has to invite me to the prom.

CHASE

You have to be on guard against the herding instinct. Can't let it creep up on you. Otherwise, the next thing you know, you're just one of the sheep.

"You sure about this?" asks Designated Dave as we roll car tires out of auto shop and into the hall.

"Who's ever sure about anything?" Ray asks.

"I didn't ask *you*, mucous brain," Dave spits. "I asked Chase."

"What's the downside?" I'm rolling three tires ahead of me. Dave and Ray each have two.

"Suspension," Dave says. "I don't want to wuss out, but BU's only given me a *provisional* acceptance. One screw up and I'm—"

"Rope won't suspend us," I tell him. "It's the spring-time of our senior year. We're expected to blow off steam. Worst case, detention."

"Yeah, you're probably right," Dave agrees uncertainly. Like he's going along with you, and he just *hopes* you're right.

We roll the tires across the main lobby and line them up at the beginning of the long, pus-green, locker-lined corridor that goes all the way down to the gym. We have seven tires, enough to span the hallway.

"How long?" I ask.

Ray checks his multifunctional digital wristwatch. "Half a minute."

"Remember, wait till the bell, then roll."

Dave's eyes dart around nervously. "I forget why we're doing this."

"Anti-herding measure."

"So?"

"Reality check. If it gives only one of them pause for reflection on the absurdity of life, then our cause is just."

"How about rolling 'em one at a time?" asks Ray. "Kinda like the bowling ball effect, you know? Pick off a few unsuspecting sheep here and there."

"I see where you're coming from, Ray," I reply. "But one at a time strikes me as borderline piecemeal. I lean toward the bulldozer approach. All at once is more like...a statement."

"You guys—" Dave shakes his head—"are totally demented."

♜

NICOLE

The two most environmentally troublesome emissions from car exhaust are carbon *monoxide* and carbon *dioxide*. In the past twenty years, thanks to unleaded gas and catalytic converters, we've made progress in the battle against smog and pollution. That's carbon *monoxide*.

But cars still produce the same amount of carbon *dioxide* as ever. As long as the world burns fossil fuels (coal, oil, and natural gas), we will continue to release billions of tons of carbon dioxide into the atmosphere every year.

Carbon dioxide is *the* major contributor to the "greenhouse effect," which causes the earth's atmosphere to get warmer. Termite flatulence is another. Termites annually produce millions of tons of methane in the form of flatulence (you know what I'm talking about).

And that's nothing compared to cow flatulence.

At the rate we're going, the human race may destroy itself by the year 2200, mostly thanks to car, termite, and cow emissions. If the Chinese decide to become middle class and start driving cars instead of riding bikes, it will happen even faster.

See? I'm not a total flake. I worry about things like that. I don't want my children's children to die of thirst and hunger on some parched patch of land like those pictures of African babies on CNN.

We have to change our lifestyles. We have to stop driving cars and start riding bikes. We have to reduce our use of electricity.

I don't know exactly what I'm going to do about it, but I know, for the sake of humanity, that I have to do something.

CHASE

You guys." Mr. Rope, our esteemed assistant principal, smirks. "Car tires."

Mr. Rope is tall and thin with fluffy gray curls that hug his head tightly. He's wearing a dark blue suit with a thread hanging out of the seam on one shoulder.

Designated Dave gives me a miserable look, clearly regretting that he ever listened to me. Dave tries very hard to be cool. He wears cool clothes and has a cool haircut. He's actually a reasonably good-looking guy with a medium-size build and a semblance of a brain.

But something in his psychological makeup prevents him from being cool. He just can't help blowing it. Maybe it's genetic.

"You guys." Mr. Rope drums his long, bony fingers on the desk like the drumroll before an execution.

Slumped in a chair with his legs crossed at the ankles, showing a lot of white sock, Ray Neely balances his square blue sunglasses on his nose. His straight brown hair is pulled into a ponytail that falls to the middle of his back. He's wearing a light blue oxford shirt and khaki pants. In his shirt pocket is a pocket protector full of pens. Around his neck is a beaded necklace with a Fender guitar pick dead center. To my knowledge, Ray doesn't play guitar.

"Car tires." Mr. Rope shakes his head and drums his fingers some more. His gaze settles on Ray.

"Us guys," says Ray.

"Right." Mr. Rope points a long, thin finger at him.

"Car tires," I add.

"Exactly." The assistant principal's finger sweeps around like a TEC 9mm machine pistol until it's aimed at me.

Designated Dave buries his face in his hands.

"Us guys." Ray starts to grin.

"You got it." Mr. Rope nods emphatically.

"Car tires," I repeat.

"Suspension?" Mr. Rope raises his eyebrows as if he's only asking. Like, he wants to see if this is a concept we can embrace.

"I'm dead," Dave moans. "It's over. My life is ruined."

NICOLE

Your father is a very, very sick man." My mother is driving me to the printer's to pick up samples for the prom invitation. It's lunchtime, but I've received special dispensation to leave school.

"You keep telling me that, Mom, but you never tell me why." Six months ago Dad moved out of our house and into an apartment on the other side of town. It didn't come as a surprise. For about a year before that I knew something was wrong. Dad was coming home really late at night and they were fighting a lot.

It sounds to me like a case of "The Other Woman," but every time I ask him or Mom, they refuse to say.

Mom stops the car at a light. A flurry of snow dulls the colors out here in the land of malls, car dealerships, and every kind of fast-food place imaginable. Mom looks over to her left at a low brick building with a gray roof and no windows. A large sign says:

PLATINUM PARADISE
ALL THIS WEEK: *Miss Beverly Hills*
AND ALWAYS 50 LOVELY YOUNG LADIES

The light turns green.
Mom's still staring.

"Mom?"

She doesn't seem to hear me. Someone behind us politely taps their car horn. Mom doesn't budge.

"Mom, the light turned green. People want to go."

The car behind us beeps more insistently.

"Mom?"

She slowly turns her head and lets our car roll forward. "Sick," she mutters.

"What?" I ask.

"Nothing."

♛

CHASE

Excuse me, Mr. Rope, but isn't the concept of punishment fitting the crime one of the cornerstones of our justice system?" I ask. "This isn't some Third World country where people are routinely caned. Are we not talking about a harmless prank? The tires have been returned to auto shop, our fellow students have moved on to their classes. Where's the harm?"

"Astute question, Chase." Mr. Rope sits back in his chair and presses the tips of his fingers together. "However, what I've begun to perceive here is the cumulative effect of an immature, yet devious, mind that has now committed a series of annoying, yet innocuous, acts designed to create disruption and disrespect toward authority in this school. The cleverness of this course of action is that no single act ever seems serious enough to merit stern discipline."

"However," I add, seeing what he's getting at, "when taken as a whole…"

Mr. Rope smiles. "You're toast."

♔

NICOLE

Alicia meets me at my locker after Mom drops me back at school. Alicia is my associate, my compatriot, my sparring partner, and my competitor. To those who don't know us well, we must appear to be great friends.

"Well?" She puts her hand on her hip and strikes a pose. Alicia is waiflike with exotic olive skin, straight black hair, large dark eyes, and a very alluring, sensual style that borders on slutsville. "Did he?"

"I told you, he's not going to." We are between periods. The hall is crowded and noisy, making it hard to hear. "At least, not directly. He can't risk it."

"I don't see why not. He *knows* you're going to say yes."

Blam! Peter Ferrat slams his locker closed, practically dislocating my ear drum.

"Do you *have* to do that?" I ask.

"Bug off, wombat." He slithers away.

"So rude!" I shout after him, then turn back to Alicia. "Nothing is certain. I'm sure he's just being careful."

Alicia rolls her eyes. "Girl Waits Lifetime for Prom Date."

Just then, from somewhere in the crowded hall, comes an ear-splitting scream. *"Alleeeeeeeeeeeeeeesha!"*

The entire hall freezes. Everyone looks around. The scream sounded either like the last plaintive cry of a dying person in love, or the yelp of a wild animal. But whoever did it remains invisible in the crowd.

A split second later, the hall lurches back to life. The decibel level quickly reaches its prior highs.

"What was *that?*" Alicia asks, bewildered.

"One of your fans." I wink.

But—" Dave's lower lip is trembling. He's really freaking out. Doesn't look cool.

"Relax, Dave. I was talking to Chase, not you," Mr. Rope informs him. "You're free to go back to class."

"I am?" Dave looks shocked.

"Just try to use your head next time. I mean, what earthly good can come out of rolling car tires down the hallway just as the bell rings?"

"Absolutely right, Mr. Rope. Never again. You can count on it." Dave pops out of his chair like a jack-in-the-box. He nods at Ray and me. "Later, dudes."

Mr. Rope turns to Ray. "And you."

"Guys." Ray grins.

"Raise those shades and come closer."

Ray raises the square blue-tinted glasses and presses up against the desk. Mr. Rope leans forward and studies his eyes. Then he nods at me. "You, too, Chase."

"Me?" He's really barking up the wrong tree.

"I need a comparison," he explains.

I do as I'm told. Mr. Rope squints into my eyes, then into Ray's. Then he presses his lips together and shakes his head. "I always forget. Are the pupils supposed to be too big, or too small?"

"Well," Ray goes. "It all depends."

⬥

NICOLE

Uh, excuse me, Alicia?" Dave Ignazzi squeezes through the crowd toward us.

"Oh, hi, Dave." Alicia turns on that alluring look she gives every male who isn't in diapers or deceased. "Was that you?"

"Who yelled? No way." Dave shakes his head. "Think I could talk to you in private for a second?"

"Uh…" Alicia's response is less than instantaneous as she jacks down the possible reasons why Designated Dave would want to speak to her. Coming up blank, curiosity takes over. She and Dave cross to the other side of the hall.

"What's with them?" a voice asks. I turn and find Chase Hammond leaning against a locker. Chase lives in the house next to mine. We've known each other since *Sesame Street*.

"Mystery," I answer.

So we wait. Chase is tall and probably good-looking under that mop of unruly brown hair. He tends to wear the same wrinkled plaid shirt and baggy olive military pants for days at a time. He and I have been close on and off over the years, but recently we've had "philosophical" differences.

A tart, yet masculine scent wafts into my nasal passages.

"Feeling a little ripe?" I ask.

Chase snorts. "You're so American, Nicole."

"Can't help it. I was born here."

"This country is totally obsessed with personal hygiene. Heaven forbid someone should smell a little. They'll be shot."

"Was that you with the tires?"

Chase shrugs. He works so hard at being an outsider. But deep inside I have a permanent soft spot for him after all those years of crawling around in the sandbox together.

"Can't find a more meaningful way to apply your energies?" I ask.

Chase smiles archly. "Sorry, Nicole, but it doesn't take me an hour to apply my makeup every morning."

"So rude!" I give him a playful shove.

"Don't worry, I won't tell anyone your deepest, darkest secrets," he teases.

Across the hall, Dave and Alicia finish their powwow. Chase and Dave go off down the corridor. Beaming, Alicia heads back toward me. "You were right! Brad asked Dave to ask me if you might be available for the prom."

I'm momentarily breathless, and practically have to fight back tears of joy. My dream is on the verge of coming true! Brad Selden is preparing to ask me to the prom! I'm so happy. As soon as the prom is over, I swear I'm going to save the whales!

♛

CHASE

Mr. Rope and I settled on a week's detention. Because of budget cutbacks, the after-hours bus has to cover half the school district, and I don't get home till dinnertime.

I step into the house. My father's sitting on the living room couch with his cowboy boots up on the only corner of the coffee table that isn't covered with CDs, magazines, or the stacks of Grateful Dead tapes he still listens to, even though Jerry's gone. He's wearing a denim shirt and jeans, and his wavy brown hair is pulled back into a ponytail. He's reading the *Wall Street Journal*.

My stomach's grumbling, so I head for the kitchen.

"Chase?" He looks up from the paper.

I stop. "Yeah?"

"Mr. Rope called."

That pukehead!

"You'll be graduating in four months. Isn't it time to grow up?"

I go into the kitchen and take a couple of foil-wrapped slices of leftover pizza out of the freezer. I'm trying to peel the stupid foil off when Dad comes in.

"Okay, you're right." He sighs. "That wasn't the best way to start a dialogue."

"I can never get the dumb foil off." Leftover pizza is a major food group in the all-male Hammond household. I've peeled away most of the foil, but little silver strips remain embedded in the frozen cheese.

"Thaw it in the microwave for a couple of seconds," he suggests.

"With the foil on it? I thought that was a clear violation of the Microwave Commandments: *Thou Shalt Not Put Metal in Thy Microwave.*"

Dad grins. "Just for a few seconds. It won't hurt."

I toss the slices in with a shrug. "It's your major appliance."

"Ray Neely was involved," says Dad.

"So?"

"You know what I'm talking about. Even Mr. Rope mentioned it."

Not this again. "Look, if Ray gets high, he doesn't tell me. Okay?"

"You're his friend, Chase."

I hold my hands out. "I voluntarily submit to a polygraph test."

"Okay, Chase, I believe you."

But deep inside I bet he doesn't.

NICOLE

My life is filled with dangerous little secrets that threaten to diminish my *P*-word-ity. It's not my dad moving out six months ago. Almost half the kids in my class have been through *that* drill.

No, these are really embarrassing secrets. Suppose, for instance, that Brad Selden were to find out that my mother is a New Age, Ziploc bag freak?

Welcome to my home, a place I try to spend as little time as possible in. Coming from the CD player is the incessant oceanic drone of New Age music that makes you feel as if you're floating on a sea of Valium. On the walls are New Age paintings of dolphins cavorting beneath a sunlit sea. We have New Age crystals and painted glass hanging in the windows, aromatherapy, and throw pillows for anyone inclined to a little impromptu meditation.

And we have Ziploc bags of every imaginable size containing almost everything that can conceivably fit in them. Food items, naturally. But also, pieces of jigsaw puzzles, pens and pencils, cotton balls, rubber bands, computer disks, plastic bottles of sunblock, old keys, loose change (divided into bags for pennies, nickels, dimes, and quarters, of course).

It's after dinner (Take-out Chinese. The little packets of soy sauce and sweet-and-sour sauce are now resting comfortably in their own little Ziploc bags, along with the left-over crispy noodles). Mom is sitting at the kitchen table clipping supermarket coupons and (you guessed it!) dividing them into Ziploc bags.

"Why so many bags, Mom?"

She sweeps her hand over the table. "Household cleaners, food, personal items."

"So that makes three bags, not nine," I point out.

"Also separated by expiration dates."

I have to discuss something serious with her. But it's best to ease into these things gently. "Can I help?"

"You clip, I'll file." Mom hands me the scissors. She is a fairly attractive woman in her late thirties. Her figure is trim and her hair is streaked blond. She works as a paralegal at the firm of Slyman and Dikemoore, (otherwise known as "Slice'em and Dice'em."), personal injury lawyers.

"So how was work today?" I ask.

She gives me a knowing glance. I'm not fooling her. "All right, how much is this going to cost me?"

Mom's lost a lot, but thank goodness she hasn't lost her sense of humor.

♛

CHASE

I t's natural selection," Ray goes. He and I are sitting at a table in the food court. Dave is over by the Orient Express, scoping a mark.

"Here's an example," Ray continues. "Let's say you're a Hun, okay? One of Attila's boys. Every time you get to a new village you slaughter, you pillage, and then what?"

"Uh, eat?" Food is on my mind.

Ray shakes his head. "It's always the big rape fest. But why?"

"'Cause you're horny?"

"Get real." Ray smirks. "You've been on the road killing people *for months*. Hardly a day goes by you don't slog around in mud, risk your life, sleep on the cold ground, if you get any sleep at all. You're dirty, hungry, and a thousand miles from home. You really believe you're gonna be thinking about nookie?"

"Well…"

"It's a species thing, Chase. Survival of the fittest. You wipe out the village and steal everything of value. That makes you stronger. Next, you impregnate the females with your genes. You're on total genetic autopilot, dude. Those genes want to make sure they get into the next generation, and you're their ticket."

I give him a funny look. "You're saying I'm not in control of my life? My *genes* are?"

"On a really basic level, absolutely."

"Yo, guys!" Dave waves. He's found a mark.

Ray and I stroll over. A woman wearing a fur jacket is in line with a tray. On one wrist she wears a gold ladies' Rolex, on the other a thick gold charm bracelet, and on her fingers are some serious stones.

"You sure there's no MSG in this?" She points through the steamy glass at the metal serving trays filled with sweet-and-sour chicken, lo mein, and beef with broccoli.

A white uniformed server on the other side of the counter shakes his head. "No MSG."

So she orders the lo mein, slides her tray toward the cashier, and pays the amazingly low lunchtime special price. Meanwhile, I've hooked up with Dave a few feet away.

"Wicked MSG buzz that stuff gave me," I say loudly.

The lady gives me a surprised look. "I just asked and they said there was no MSG."

"Yeah, right." I tremble and shake a little. "Then how come I'm breaking out in a sweat and feeling tingly all over?"

The lady narrows her eyes. You can almost see the debate in her head. Should she go back and make a scene about returning the lo mein? Or just dump it and grab a frozen yogurt?

She heads for the garbage can. Ray's hovering nearby, looking hungry.

"Excuse me," he goes. "You're not really gonna throw that out, are you?"

NICOLE

We all have our tragedies. Mine is that I was not born with natural beauty or a svelte figure. My ankles are thick, my legs are unshapely, my hips do not curve, and my chest is less than ample. Without makeup my face is plain. Left on its own, my dirty-blond hair tends to curl and creep down my shoulders like some wild jungle vine.

But I've learned to compensate—streaking my hair and taming it with hours of brushing and blow-drying. Applying makeup in ways that are not immediately obvious. Choosing my clothes selectively and dressing with great care.

I spend a great deal of time trying to *maximize* my appearance and, given what I have to work with, I am reasonably proud of the result.

My father is also proud of me. At least, that's what he says. Last week at the movies he seemed sad and I asked him why.

"Because I don't see you enough," he said.

"Then come home," I said.

"I can't."

So I asked why and he just looked melancholy and shook his head. "I'm sorry, hon. You wouldn't understand."

I didn't get mad. I'm beyond that. For months before he moved out—when it was obvious that something was wrong—I begged and pleaded, yelled and screamed, even threatened to run away if they didn't tell me what was going on. But neither of them would say a word.

Finally, one night when Dad was allegedly "working late," I called his office. Someone there told me he'd left work hours ago.

"Look, Mom," I said. "We both know he's not at work. He doesn't go to sporting events. He hates to shop and he doesn't drink. So for Pete's sake, will you just tell me where he is?"

My mother gazed sadly at me and said, "in ecstacy."

She never explained what she meant. Now, the divorce is costing both of them a fortune. Needless to say, Mom hasn't had positive feelings about my father or any other man for quite a while.

"Men," she goes, "are a disease."

"Brad Selden's going to ask me to the prom." I clip a Vaseline Intensive Care lotion with an August expiration.

"When?" Mom files the coupon in the appropriate Ziploc bag.

"Soon, I hope."

"No, I meant, when is the prom?"

"June, why?"

"Because it's the middle of February."

"It's like fruit, Mom. The ripe ones go first."

Mom looks up and gazes across the yard. We can see into the Hammonds' kitchen. Chase's dad, Rob, is sitting at his kitchen table eating dinner by himself.

Mom turns back to me. "Which one's Brad?"

"The tall, really good-looking one. Plays center for the basketball team. Remember, I pointed him out at the game?"

"The one who kept missing?"

"He's much better on defense."

Mom smiles crookedly. "I'm glad he's found his niche."

I take a deep breath. "Anyway, it's going to cost money."

"The dress, the hair…" Mom scowls. "What else?"

"Tickets."

The spidery lines around her eyes deepen. "What about Brad?"

"He'll pay for the limo."

"Limo?"

"It's a safety thing."

"How about I drive and you pay me?"

I roll my eyes.

"Still, how much could the limo cost?" she asks.

"It's for twenty-four hours. The pre-prom parties, the prom, the post-prom parties, and the beach."

"I see."

"So what do you think?"

"I think you better clip a lot of coupons between now and June."

That explains the whole popularity thing," Ray says. We're sitting at a small table which, along with four chairs, is bolted to the food court floor lest any table thieves try walking off with it. On three paper plates, we've divided the lo mein into equal portions.

Dave looks up. "Did I miss something?"

"Ray's been explaining popularity in terms of Attila the Hun."

"Huh?" Dave frowns.

"Instinct," Ray says. "People don't even know why they need to be popular. They just do. The most beautiful and the brightest are drawn together in an orgy of genetic coupling. Natural selection. Survival of the fittest."

"Lame." Dave shakes his head dismissively.

"Maybe he's onto something," I counter.

"Onto? Or just plain *on?*" Dave presses his fingers to his lips and pretends to inhale deeply on a blunt.

"Look at yourself, Dave," Ray says. "You jump out of bed in the middle of the night to chauffeur drunk jocks around. What do you think *that's* all about?"

"It's not just jocks, dimwad," Dave snaps. "It's anyone too wasted to drive. We're talking about saving lives."

"Aw, my hero." Ray smirks. "And all this time I thought it was just an excuse to hang with the cool kids."

Dave loads a plastic fork with rice, bends it back, and catapults it at Ray.

Who ducks.

The flying rice sails toward this big biker dude sitting behind us. It hits him in the back of the neck, and then slides down inside his shirt.

"Hey!" The guy spins around. His head is shaved and he has a scraggly goatee, serious nose piercings, and a denim shirt with the sleeves ripped off. Tattoos of vipers, naked women, and a black panther festoon his massive arms.

Looks like it's time to bail.

♔

NICOLE

Alicia fascinates me. Her father is an executive for a multi-national corporation. He gets transferred every two or three years, and as a result, Alicia has lived all over the world. After we graduate, she's going to Europe for the summer, and then staying abroad to study fashion in Paris. To a home-body like me it sounds frightening, but to Alicia it's simply more of the same.

We're trying on clothes in my bedroom. The contrast of Alicia's smooth olive skin against her white lacy brassiere is almost breathtaking. She is one-quarter Asian, one-quarter Native American, and one-half Caucasian. The result is an exotic beauty that every girl in our class, with the possible exception of Chloe Frost, envies.

"Then why don't the boys like me?" she asks, spinning on her toes in front of my closet mirror to check out the back of her new jeans.

"Jason does," I remind her. She and Jason Rooney, one of the football players, have been on again/off again since Alicia moved here in tenth grade.

"I meant, the *other* boys."

"They're intimidated."

"I thought Chloe's the one who intimidates them."

"It's different. Chloe intimidates them with maturity and sophistication. You intimidate them with raw animal sexuality."

"Really?" Alicia's eyes sparkle with delight. "BOYS QUIVER AT RAW ANIMAL APPEAL."

Another thing about Alicia—she thinks in checkout counter headlines.

"Have you and Jason talked prom yet?" I ask.

Alicia shakes her head.

"How come?"

She shrugs her slim, naked shoulders. In the summer she wears bikinis the size of friendship bracelets.

"Have we entered nonverbal mode?" I ask.

"It hasn't come up."

"Don't you think you should bring it up?"

"Maybe."

"What does that mean?"

"It's the spring of our senior year, Nicole. Pretty soon this will all be but a memory. GIRL LEAVES PAST, EMBRACES FUTURE."

I find Alicia's attitude amazing. To me, having worked so hard to achieve my current status, high school is everything. I don't look forward to the end of school. If anything, I *dread* it. It lacks form, shape, and structure. Life after high school is an abyss.

To avoid capture one must sometimes resist the temptation to flee. While Ray and Dave sprint off in opposite directions, I stop at a card table set up near the food court and pretend to read some literature lying there. A large, bluish plastic watercooler bottle is chained to the table. Some dollar bills and change lay at the bottom.

"Chase?" A hushed voice whispers.

I look up into the amber-green eyes of Dulcie Wheaton, seated behind the coffee table. A red and white *Pro Choice* button is pinned to her sleeveless white blouse.

"Don't turn around," she whispers. "He's right behind you."

Not moving a muscle, I stare down at a petition on the table.

"Maybe you'd like to sign this while you're waiting," Dulcie suggests. "We're lobbying to loosen restrictions against RU-486."

I pick up a pen. "What's that?"

"The morning-after pill. It induces a spontaneous miscarriage. The French have been using it for years, but state and federal restrictions make it almost impossible to get here."

"Figures." I sign the petition.

"Good news." Dulcie's voice returns to normal. "He's gone."

I glance out of the corner of my eye and see the biker dude down by Bed, Bath, and Beyond hulking away.

"Thanks, Dulce." I straighten up.

"Anytime." Dulcie's thick, curly black hair falls over her shoulders. You never see her without a cause. I had a crush on her from about sixth to ninth grade. At parties we'd dance or make out. But just when I thought things would get serious, she changed. Except for school, I hardly ever see her anymore.

"So this is what you're into these days?" I gesture at the literature.

Dulcie gives me a bemused look. "You mean, like a fad? Last week, Rollerblades; this week, RU-486?" She's always had a teasing sense of humor.

"You know what I meant."

"Unwanted pregnancies are a horribly serious problem, Chase. It puts stress on so many overburdened social services—medicine, education, the penal system, welfare. So much could be solved just by taking one little pill."

"Wow, sounds so good, maybe _I_ should take one."

Dulcie doesn't smile. "It's not funny."

"Okay, okay, it was just a joke." I reach forward and slide my fingers through her thick beautiful hair. "Maybe I'll come by one of these days."

Dulcie's eyes sparkle. "Okay."

"Chase?" Dave comes up behind me and sees her. "Oh, hi, Dulcie."

"Hi, Dave."

He turns to me. "Think we better get while the getting's good."

"See ya." I give Dulcie a wave and get a smile back.

Dave and I head out. "You seen Ray?" I ask.

"No."

"Don't you think we ought to make sure he's okay?"

"No."

I stop and look back. There's no sign of him down the wide store-lined promenade of the mall. "Don't be a jerk, Dave."

"Look who's talking."

"What's your problem?"

"Guy's a cretin."

"He's my friend."

"Hey, everyone makes a mistake."

NICOLE

One of the reasons my mother's legal bills are so high is that it took about three months just for her and Dad to agree on when he could see me. She absolutely insisted that I be with her on all the major holidays. She also insisted that he not come to any school function—such as commencement and the Grand March at the prom—that she might attend. Basically, she never wants to see him again.

As far as visitation, they finally agreed that I would spend every other Sunday with him as well as dinner on Wednesday nights.

"Either your dad has a really cheesy lawyer or he's into something mega-spicy," said Alicia.

Sitting in Pizza Hut with Dad, it's hard to imagine him into anything even remotely "spicy." As I said, this is a man with almost no hobbies or interests outside of work. He's sort of scrawny, and always looks pale and tired. More than a day's worth of grayish stubble on his jaw makes him appear unkempt. He used to be bald and wear thick glasses. Then about a year ago, he went out and got a bad-fitting toupee that looks more like roadkill than a hairpiece. More recently he got contact lenses, which make his eyes red and watery.

"How are you?" he asks, leaning his elbows on the table and blinking.

"Okay, Dad. You?"

"Okay, I guess."

"Is this the day you finally tell me what's going on?"

Dad looks at me with those red, watery eyes and shakes his head. "I'm sorry, Nicky, honey."

"Are you *ever* going to tell me?"

He raises his hands in a helpless gesture.

"It's not an illness or anything, is it?" I'm thinking *AIDS*.

"Well, no, hon, not the way you mean it."

"What's *that* mean?" Now I'm even more puzzled.

Dad reaches across the table and puts his hand over mine. "I am truly sorry to have to keep you in the dark like this. Believe me, I wouldn't do this if I didn't have to."

"But why?" I ask. "I don't get it."

"I'm sorry, hon. I'm really, truly sorry."

"Okay, how about this. Are you happy or sad?"

"Every once in a while happy. Mostly sad."

"And you want it this way?"

"Yes. It's…almost beyond my control."

"Dad, *please?*"

"I can't, Nicky. Believe me, I love you more than anything, and it kills me to leave you in the dark. But I don't have a choice. Please try to understand."

As much as I'd like to, I can't hate this man.

♛

CHASE

Mr. Rope leans forward on his desk and interlocks his fingers. "Just what is it that you're fighting against, Chase?"

I'm in his office again, charged with another minor offense—chronic tardiness to class.

"The Pavlovian nature of public education," I reply.

"Excuse me?"

"You know the experiment Pavlov did with dogs, where he got them to salivate at the sound of a bell because he always rang the bell when he was going to feed them?" I ask.

"Yes."

"Well, the kids in this school are the same way."

Mr. Rope raises an eyebrow. "They drool when the bell rings?"

"They're automatons. They *know* when the bell's going to ring. It's programmed into their biological clocks. Every forty minutes they reach for their backpacks and start to get up. It's a reflex."

"So's giving you detention."

I leave the office and go into the boys' room. Smells like pizza. That means that Jeff Branco is in the last stall with a bunch of pizzas a friend of his copped from some place downtown. Jeff sells the slices for two dollars each.

Ray's slouched outside the stall door with his hands jammed in his pockets.

"Aw, come on, Jeff," he whines.

"Forget it!" Jeff barks from inside the stall.

"I swear I'll pay you back."

"Get lost, Neely."

"How about a trade?" Ray suggests.

"Not interested."

"Jeez, some friend."

"If I want friends like you, I'll hang out at the Betty Ford Rehab Center."

Ray's shoulders sag and he swivels his head toward me. "Help me out, Chase?"

"Uh…" I stall. Ray never pays you back. You'd have better luck betting that this country will ban handguns.

"What about it, Chase?" Ray practically begs. "I haven't eaten in *days*."

"Don't do it, Chase," Jeff calls from inside the stall.

"What do you care, Jeff?" I call back. "You'll get your money either way."

"It's the principle of the thing," Jeff says.

"Principle?" I ask.

"If he says he's gonna pay you back, he should mean it. If he's just gonna stiff you, he should be up front about it."

Jeez, everyone's so righteous these days.

The bathroom door swings open and Chester the Custodian lunges in, pushing a mop and a gray metal bucket on wheels. We're talking Major Hippie Anachronism here: Walks in this weird, gimpy way. Rail thin, gray hair parted in the middle, red bandanna around his forehead, wornout jeans, droopy mustache, a peace sign tattooed on his forearm, turquoise and silver bracelet on one wrist, permanently glazed eyes. The Ghost of Cannabis Past. Humming some ancient Grateful Dead song. He stops and sniffs. A big grin appears revealing gaps of missing teeth. "Mr. Branco, my man, do I sense your presence?"

"That you, Chester?" Jeff calls from inside the stall.

"Last time I checked. So, my fine delinquent friend, can you spare one?"

"For you? Anytime."

Chester gimps down to the last stall. Jeff slides out a slice on a paper plate.

"Hey! That's not fair!" Ray cries. "*He* didn't have to pay!"

"Professional courtesy," Jeff replies.

One of the biggest challenges in a girl's life is getting boys to do what they're supposed to do. Occasionally, a boy won't do something because he actually doesn't want to. But most of the time they don't do it because they simply don't have a clue.

Yes, the simple truth is: Boys are incredibly thick. All they think about is sports and issues related to the removal of female undergarments. Do you think there'd be a prom if it was up to *them?*

Of course not. Which is why I'm the chairman of the prom planning committee. The PPC is (and I'm not trying to brag) the elite of our class. We are the core decision makers. Most of us are on other committees and have seats in the class government. Once a week at lunch we meet to eat, make prom arrangements, and gossip.

Today Chloe Frost, who's in charge of finding a prom band, has tapes of three bands. We arrange the desks in a circle and listen on a boom box.

We all agree that the Genital Warts are by far the best, but we can't hire them because of their name.

"That leaves Bonehead Ted and the Surf Snotwads, or The Wipes," says Chloe.

"Aren't there any other choices?" I ask.

Chloe shakes her head. "Everyone else is already booked or beyond our budget."

I glance around at the rest of the committee. "Anyone have a preference?"

No one budges.

"Maybe we should see what they look like," Alicia suggests.

We all agree that's a good idea. Chloe says she'll get pictures of both groups.

"What about the Grand March issue?" asks Sandy Kimmel, who's in charge of refreshments.

The Grand March is a tradition at Timothy Zonin (otherwise known as Time Zone) High. Prom is actually short for promenade, or grand entrance. At the start of the prom, the cafeteria is filled with parents and relatives. Each couple enters from the back and walks down a central red carpet, while the prom song plays, and everyone cheers and takes pictures. Even though the Grand March comes first in the evening, it is truly the highlight of the night, the moment when everyone wants to look their best.

And the best always comes last.

In the 1960s, Time Zone High abolished the King and Queen of the prom. Since then it has been a tradition of the Grand March that the last dozen or so couples to enter the cafeteria are always the most popular. And even within that final dozen there is supposedly an order, so that the Absolute Most Popular couples are the very last.

Sandy Kimmel, whose date for the prom is in doubt, wants to abolish the Grand March. The rest of us exchange dubious glances.

"It's been a tradition since forever," I point out. Of course, as Brad Selden's date, I have a virtual lock on being among the last few couples.

"I tend to side with Nicole," agrees Chloe, even though she's going out with some college guy she met during the community theater production of *Bye-Bye Birdie*. Since he's an outsider, the best Chloe can hope for is to be in the final dozen.

"Me, too," adds Alicia. "And, like, has *anyone* been asked yet?"

Chloe raises her hand sheepishly.

"We already know about you, Chloe," Alicia says. "Anyone else?"

"Eddie's going to take Bo," I observe.

"Dee," Chloe reminds me. "She changed her name, remember?"

Eddie Lampel is the quarterback of the football team. Dee, formerly Bo, Vine is someone who had always been in the shadows but has recently come on strong, making them contenders for the Final Four.

"Any word on Kyle?" I ask.

Chloe shrugs. She and Kyle Winthrop went out for years, but that's over now.

"I heard he's seeing someone from another school," says Sandy. That will put him in the top dozen, but no better.

"What's the latest on Brad?" Chloe asks me.

"I've received a preliminary inquiry," I reply. "Everything appears to be on course."

CHASE

I *swear* I'll pay you back," Ray insists. "I mean it. Soon as I get some bucks, they're yours."

"Your mother's grave?" I ask.

"Cross my heart."

I pull some bills out of my pocket and slide them under the stall door. Two slices come out on paper plates. Ray takes one and I take the other.

"Neely's a leech," Jeff says from inside. "I don't understand you, Chase."

"Yeah, well, join the crowd," I reply.

Ray and I leave the boys' room carrying our half-eaten slices on our paper plates.

"You're a good man, Chase," Ray says through a mouthful.

"Oh? That means my genes are gonna survive while those around me perish?"

"Probably not." Ray takes another bite. "Selfishness rules today's world. It's look out for numero uno. That's why it was really nice of you to buy me this slice, but in the long run that kind of behavior'll probably finish you."

"So maybe I wouldn't want to be around in that kind of world, anyway."

"Yeah, exactly." Ray holds out his hand and I give him a high five.

At the current rate of global warming, all the beaches on the East Coast of the United States will disappear in about twenty-five years. In the meantime, my mother has finally allowed me to take a job becoming of a person of my stature. She's never let me do anything more serious than baby-sit before. She insisted it was because my after-school hours should be dedicated to homework. But that's a joke. More recently, she admitted that she simply couldn't stand the idea of me working in some fast-food place where her friends might come in and see me. Of course, just what her friends would be doing in such a place is another story entirely.

But she finally relents when I tell her I want to tutor little kids. After all, it's a good cause. And it pays.

"That's almost what I make an hour!" she gasps, wide-eyed.

"Life is a career path." I shrug.

"How did you get the job?" she asks.

I was afraid she'd ask that. The truth is, Dad arranged it after I told him I needed to make money for the prom.

Briiiiiinnnnnng! The wall phone rings. Mom gets it. "Oh, hi, Rob."

It's Chase's dad. I look across the yard and see him standing by his kitchen window, one hand holding the phone while waving at us with the other.

"A cup of milk?" Mom says. "Of course. I'll send Nicole over with it."

Groan. When do we stop being our parents' little messengers?

"Oh, okay, if you insist." Mom hangs up and checks her hair in the reflection of the microwave. "He's coming here. Poor man. It must be hard to raise a boy alone."

"Any harder than raising a girl alone?"

"At least I keep the refrigerator filled." Mom opens the fridge and takes out the milk. It appears that she's forgotten about the tutoring job.

Lucky me.

Dave thinks Ray's full of crap, but I'm intrigued. The guy *thinks*. He's not part of the herd. Sometimes I feel like we're all living in an ant farm, working like mad at being cool and popular and whatever. But no matter what we do, we're never gonna get past the glass walls. But Ray...he's out there looking in at us. How does he do it?

I walk into the kitchen. Smells like eggs cooking. The CD player is on loud, blasting this 1960s Cream song called "Crossroads." My father is standing next to the stove, eyes closed, fingers wriggling up and down some air-guitar's invisible fretboard. He's shaking his head and his ponytail slaps back and forth like a horse swatting flies.

I clear my throat. "Can I ask you something?"

Eric Clapton opens his eyes. "Oh, whatsup, Chase?" He smiles sheepishly.

"Instead of spending your whole life being some kind of wanna-be, why don't you really learn to play?"

Dad gives me a wistful look. "Time, Chase."

"Make the time."

"Right. I bet there's a big demand for middle-aged novice guitar players right now. Maybe I'll just let the company go, sell the house, and hit the road."

Dad started his own computer software company about five years ago, not that he knows anything about computers.

He just hires people who do. Dad lifts a pan off the stove. "Western omelet?"

"Sure."

He slides the omelet out of the pan and onto a plate, then slides the plate in front of me. "OJ?"

"Thanks."

He takes a pitcher out of the fridge and pours me a glass, humming.

"You're in a good mood."

"Got that right."

"What's the occasion?"

"Possibilities, Chase." He cracks some more eggs in a bowl.

It's probably some profitable development with his business. Meanwhile, I notice a new book on the kitchen table. *Woodstock Generation: A Photographic Memory.* Dad's always buying books about the sixties and hippies and stuff. Except for the occasional omelet, he's your basic granola-oriented 1960s relic. Marched against the war in Vietnam, drove around in a psychedelic VW bus, and slopped in the mud at Woodstock.

I thumb through the book. Here's a page showing some hippie with long, shaggy hair and a beard puffing on a joint rolled out of American flag paper.

Wait a minute!

He's always acting suspicious about *me* taking drugs....

"Hey, Dad, *you* ever take drugs?"

That stops him cold. He turns toward me, holding up an empty egg shell. "This is your brain, Chase." *Crunch!* He crushes the shell in his hand. "This is your brain on drugs."

"Serious, Dad."

"So am I." He dumps the crushed shell in the sink and rinses off his hand.

"Don't get me wrong, Dad, but I don't get it. You looked like a hippie, you went to Woodstock, and you never smoked pot?"

"I *tried* it," he allows.

"And?"

"Made me dizzy."

"That's it?"

"Uh-huh." He puts the pan on the stove and pours himself some coffee.

"No one puts a gun to your head."

"*That's* what I keep telling you, but you never believe me."

Smoke starts to rise out of the omelet pan.

"Hey, pay attention," I tell him.

"Damn." He swings the pan under the faucet and hits it with a blast of water. *Sizzle*. Steam rises.

"Rattled?" I can't help smiling.

Dad levels a serious gaze at me. "I knew people who died because of drugs."

Is that, like, a threat?

NICOLE

I guess I inherited my math genes from my father. It always comes amazingly easy to me. Algebra? No sweat. Geometry? Piece of cake. Trigonometry? Maybe a few minutes a night of serious concentration.

"As far as I'm concerned, you're more than just a tutor," Stacy tells me. "You're also a role model."

When Stacy met me at the door, it really caught me off guard. I'm not exactly tall, but I tower over her. Stacy can't even break five feet. She adds four inches in teased-up bleached-blond hair, and also has some of the longest fingernails I've ever seen, each painted bright red and finely honed. I would guess that she's in her mid-to-late twenties.

Now we're sitting in the kitchen. Callie, Stacy's nine-year-old daughter (brown hair, bangs), is in the den watching TV. Stacy wants to make sure I understand the gravity of the situation.

"I think it's really important that Callie not be exposed to stereotyping," she goes on. "Women can be good at math."

"I know."

Stacy studies me. "You are?"

"Uh, yeah, that's why I'm here."

Her smile has a brittle quality to it. "I wish I was."

The kitchen is so clean, it looks *polished*. There's hardly a surface you can't see yourself in. Who does the scrubbing? Not Stacy with those fingernails. She slides a cigarette out of a pack, lights up, and takes a puff. Interesting juxtaposition—a woman concerned about stereotypes, who keeps a kitchen that sparkles, and who smokes.

"I've talked to Callie's teacher about this," she goes on. "At some point it would probably be a good idea for you to talk to her, too. But for now, it's really important that Callie not feel like there's anything wrong with her, because there isn't. Everyone's good at some things and bad at others. I want my daughter to feel that she can be as good as you are at math. Only it may take her a little more work."

"Sure." Sounds reasonable to me.

Stacy studies me again. Ever since I stepped into the house, I've felt like I've been under a microscope. "You spend a lot of time with your dad?"

"Not since he moved out."

She nods, takes another puff.

"He didn't exactly explain how he knew you," I add.

Stacy replies tersely: "Business."

♛

CHASE

Dulcie and I are on her couch. Actually, Dulcie is on my lap. She's leaning back against the arm of the couch, gazing up at me with this dreamy look in her eyes while her fingers twirl my hair. No one's home and we've been making out for a good half an hour.

Not that anything serious has gone down. Dulcie's made it clear that it's not *that* kind of relationship. But she likes to hug and kiss. And since I've always liked her, I don't mind, even though it leaves me feeling kind of frustrated.

"What are you thinking?" she asks.

About what it might be like if she was a little more accommodating. But I can't tell her that. "Uh, nothing."

"You won't tell?"

"Maybe there's nothing to tell."

"Liar." She taps my forehead with her finger. "I know there's a lot going on in there."

She won't give up until I tell her *something*. So I blurt out the first thing that comes to mind. "I think my father used to do drugs."

"What!?" Dulcie's eyes widen.

"Not like an addict or anything, but like when he was in high school and college. Recreational stuff."

"Why do you think that?"

I tell her how he used to go to Grateful Dead concerts

and dressed like a hippie and hung around with hippies. "Mostly it's because he's so suspicious of *me*."

"Takes one to know one?"

"You got it."

"So?" Dulcie says.

"It bothers me."

"Why?"

"If he did use drugs, then he's lying when he says he didn't. And where does he get off telling me not to?"

"Have you asked him?"

"Yeah. He basically says he didn't inhale."

"Maybe that's true."

"Gimme a break, Dulce. I know him. He's afraid that if he tells me the truth, it's like giving me permission to do it, too."

"Would you?"

"Good question."

Dulcie looks straight into my eyes. "You know, people already suspect…because of Ray."

"I've never seen him touch anything. I swear."

Dulcie rolls her eyes in disbelief. "Oh, come on, Chase."

"Maybe he's just that way naturally."

"You can't be that naive."

"Hey, which of us hangs out with him, huh? I'd know."

Dulcie shifts her weight. "So you're thinking about it?"

"I don't know. Maybe. Who knows?"

She sits up and slides off my lap. All of a sudden she's looking very serious. "Why, Chase?"

"Well…" I shrug. "I mean, when your old man already *thinks* you do…"

Dulcie's forehead wrinkles. "What happened to you?"

What's she talking about? "I don't know. Maybe you better tell me."

"You always had so much potential. But it's like you won't grow up and get serious. You're still getting into trouble all the time and acting like you're in eighth grade."

Ouch! That hurt. Now I remember what makes me both love and hate Dulcie. She always says exactly what's on her mind, and she doesn't seem to care whether you like it or not.

"Gee, Dulce, who named you the high priestess of righteousness?"

She shakes her head sadly. "No one, Chase."

How's the tutoring?" Mom asks. The house smells icky sweet.

"Okay. What's that smell?"

"Lavender. It helps relieve stress. You're going to be a rich young lady soon."

Brriiiiiiinnngggg! The phone. I answer it.

"Sit down." It's Alicia.

"Why?"

"Just sit."

"Okay." I'm still standing.

"Are you sitting?"

I'm getting annoyed. "Would you just tell me what this is about?"

"You really have to sit," Alicia insists.

"Are you sure you don't mean beg?"

"Okay, have it your way." Alicia takes a dramatic pause. "Brad asked Dulcie Wheaton to the prom."

I sit down, hard. "This is a joke, right?"

"Do I tell jokes?" Alicia asks.

She has a point.

CHASE

She's gotta be here somewhere." Friday afternoon at Dave's. He's on-line, surfing chat rooms, looking for some girl who's supposed to live over in Elmsdale. Tonight Dave, Ray, and I are supposed to get together with her and her friends.

"You won't believe this babe," Dave says. "If she's a tenth as hot as she says she is, we're blessed."

Ray and I share a dubious look. That's a major *if.*

"Bingo!" Dave, whose screen name is Ignaz, starts typing:

> IGNAZ: HEY, HOT, WASN'T SURE YOU'D SHOW.
>
> HOT2TROT: SORRY, MY LITTLE BRO WAS HOGGING THE HARDWARE.
>
> IGNAZ: YOU STILL ON FOR TONIGHT?
>
> HOT2TROT: OH, YEAH.;-)

"Cool!" Dave gasps. "See, guys? I wasn't making it up!"

> IGNAZ: I'VE GOT MY FRIENDS, CHASE AND RAY. YOU GOT YOURS?
>
> HOT2TROT: DEFINITELY.
>
> IGNAZ: TIME AND PLACE?
>
> HOT2TROT: JUNIOR HIGH PARKING LOT. MIDNIGHT.

IGNAZ: YOU MEAN, THE MIDDLE SCHOOL?

HOT2TROT: RIGHT. YOU AND YOUR FRIENDS BETTER BE HUNKS.

IGNAZ: BELIEVE IT. AND YOU AND YOURS ARE BABES, RIGHT?

HOT2TROT: JUST YOU WAIT.;-)

IGNAZ: MIDNIGHT IT IS.

HOT2TROT: CAN'T WAIT. BYE.

Dave signs off and claps his hands together. "This is it, dudes! Our dream come true!"

"David!" Mrs. Ignazzi calls from downstairs. "Dinner-time!"

"Just a minute!" Dave calls back, then turns to us. "Okay, guys, we'll meet back here at ten."

"Uh, what're we gonna do between now and ten?" Ray asks.

Dave takes a deep sniff. "Smells kind of pungent in here. How about doing something really unusual...like take a shower?"

"Don't have to," Ray says.

Dave knits his brow and looks pissed. "Look, dirtbag, this isn't just about you, okay? It's about me and Chase, too. You want to blow it for us?"

"Don't sweat, man, I won't smell," Ray says.

"How are you going to manage that?" Dave asks.

Ray points at his head. "Mind over matter."

Dave rolls his eyes. "Right. Only you have no mind, and it doesn't seem to matter."

The average cow releases 50 to 100 gallons of methane *per day*. Cow methane production amounts to 50 million metric tons a year worldwide. Besides being a major contributor to the greenhouse effect, methane is highly flammable. There are reports of cows spontaneously combusting.

Why am I thinking about this? Desperate times call for desperate measures. After some quick detective work, I learn that Brad is playing cards at Eddie Lampel's house. To intrude is unthinkable, but I'm tempted just the same. If I can get my hands on an Uzi, I'll do more than intrude.

Short of an Uzi, maybe I can find an exploding cow.

In the kitchen, Mom looks up from her astrology column. "Something wrong?"

"I hate men," I mutter.

She puts down the newspaper and presses her lips together. "It's my fault. All the anger I've vented at your father has been a bad influence."

"It has nothing to do with that. Boys are completely undependable, unreliable, and have no sense of decency."

"I'd say that was true of *most* of them," Mom says. "Not all."

I give her a curious look. "Are we changing our tune?"

CHASE

Twenty minutes past midnight.

The middle school parking lot.

One car.

Three idiots, myself included.

Dave reeks of cologne. He's wearing enough of the stuff to neutralize a locker room.

Ray is lying on his back on the car hood, staring up at the dark, moonless sky.

Dave looks at his watch. "Ten more minutes. That's it. I swear."

"Right." I let out a sigh.

"I bet she's lost," Dave says.

"Right."

"Chase, you don't know this girl. I've been talking to her for weeks. She's gonna show."

"Right."

Still lying on his back, Ray points upward. "Know what that is?"

I look up. The sky is awash with sparkling stars. "The Big Dipper?"

"I mean that fuzzy belt of light that gets fat right over our heads."

I see what he means. "What?"

"The Milky Way, man. Our very own galaxy."

Even Dave looks up. "Serious?"

"Believe it. We're out on the edge, so we can see into the middle. That fuzzy stuff is millions and millions of stars."

"You sure it's not a cloud?" Dave asks.

"No way," I say. "It doesn't even look like a cloud."

"Wow." Dave sounds truly in awe. "So that's the Milky Way."

"Millions of stars," Ray goes. "And millions of planets just like ours. And it's so big, man. Bigger than we can ever truly comprehend. Even the fastest space vehicle would take millions and millions of years to reach the other side."

For a moment we're all silent. I mean, the vastness of the whole thing...it makes us so small in comparison. A tiny grain of sand in a huge ocean. What an awesome thing to think about.

Ray finally breaks the silence. "And just think, man. They named the whole thing after a candy bar."

Dave groans and shakes his head. "Why do I listen to you?"

"So what about it, Ray?" I ask.

"There's life out there," Ray says. "I mean, if it can happen here, then somewhere out there is another planet where there just *has* to be another form of life."

"Probably," Dave mutters. "Because that must be where *you* came from."

"I think it's reasonable to assume there's life out there," I agree.

"Think about this," Ray says. "Wherever that life is, and no matter what form it takes, it's the same scene. Natural selection. Survival of the fittest."

"Here we go again," Dave grumbles.

"Back off," I warn him.

Ray sits up on the car hood. "See, just because we've evolved a little, we have this weird idea that we're not animals anymore. So much of what humans do is based on this pretense that we're superior. Like just because we've got clothes, manners, and schools, we think we're better."

"What's he raving about now?" Dave asks.

"I don't know, Dave," I shoot back. "But it sure beats waiting for Little Miss Hot2Trot to not show."

"It's all about natural selection," Ray goes on. "The better we dress, the more manners we have, the more educated we are—it's all supposed to guarantee that our genes will have a better shot at surviving into future generations. But it's like, all warped."

"*You're* all warped," Dave mutters.

Ray starts tracing a figure eight in the air over and over again. "We're tadpoles, man, thrashing around in this little puddle of life like there's some reason behind it. Like we're trying to get somewhere. But it's just a loop, man, a figure eight. Maybe each generation evolves a little more than the last, but we're still covering the same territory. You get a little smarter, a little less hair grows on your body, they make a faster computer chip, but nothing really changes."

"It's still survival of the fittest?" I think I see where he's going.

"You got it, Chase."

"Well, you're about as unfit as they come, douche brain," Dave snaps at him. "So where does that leave you?"

Ray hangs his head. Sometimes Dave really pisses me off. "Lay off him." I get in his face.

"Or what?" Dave doesn't budge.

This is ridiculous. I've got four inches and thirty pounds on him. We both know I can cream him. But then what? Then I'm doing the same thing to him that he does to Ray.

I take a deep breath and let it out slow. "Look, Dave, I'm truly sorry Little Miss Hot2Trot jerked you around, okay? But don't take it out on Ray. It's not his fault."

Dave's jaw sags. I'm pretty sure I caught him by surprise. He backs off, and nods.

Beep…beep…beep. His beeper goes off. He checks the phone number and heaves a sigh. "Lampel's house. Might as well do some good tonight."

NICOLE

I've staked my place in the dark at the foot of Brad's driveway. As someone who tries to maintain herself as the ultimate in *P*-word, this probably isn't constructive behavior. But for once I'm beyond caring. Brad has put me in an untenable position. No matter how hard I try, I can't think of an alternative male of acceptable quality who is still available to accompany me on the penultimate event of my high school career.

Brad clearly doesn't understand the ramifications of what he's done. He's brought me to the brink of the greatest humiliation of my life! Asking Dulcie instead of me has to be some kind of joke, a goof, a whim. He can't be serious.

He has to take me to the prom. He simply *has* to!

Headlights are coming around the corner. It's Designated Dave. I can't let him see me.

Crouching behind a bush next to Brad's driveway, I'm feeling more nervous than the first time I addressed the entire student body in the auditorium. I take a deep breath and try to relax, reminding myself that I have to remain calm and logical. Since I can't *force* him to change his mind, I have to be sweet and wonderful and *show* him why it's in both our best interests.

The car turns into the driveway. The door opens and six-feet-four-inch Brad unfolds out, along with a mist of cologne so strong, I can smell it ten feet away.

"Thanks, Dave."

"Sure you can make it into the house?" Dave asks from inside the car. "I could come in and make you some coffee."

"That's really nice of you, but I'll be okay." Brad closes the door.

Dave backs the car out of the driveway.

I rise from behind the bush.

"Ah!" Brad lets out a cry.

Neither Ray nor I feel like accompanying Dave on his mission to save drunk jocks. Instead, we walk home under the Milky Way.

"What's with that guy?" Ray asks.

"Who?"

"Designated 'Dip' Dave."

"I don't know, Ray."

"He's a downer."

"Sometimes."

Ray kicks a rock and it skids off the road shoulder and into the brush. "Why do you hang with him?"

"He's not so bad. He's just trying to figure it all out like the rest of us. He copes his way, you cope yours."

We walk a little more, kick a few more rocks and a flattened can or two. Ray's hands are jammed into his pockets. His hair's down and I can just see the tip of his nose.

"Does it get to you, Chase?"

"Huh?"

"The absurdity. I mean, don't you ever feel like, why bother?"

"Lack of alternatives, Ray."

"Sometimes...sometimes I wonder."

I stop and stare at him in the dark. "For real?"

Ray shrugs. "Yes and no."

"That's serious, bud."

"You never?" He gives me a curious look.

"Not seriously," I tell him. "The finality's too grue-some."

We start to walk again. "What about when it gets bad?" he asks.

"I try to get through it and go on to something better."

"How do you know there'll be something better?"

Good point. "I don't. I just assume."

"So it's your outlook," Ray observes.

"But it's true, isn't it? Something better usually comes along. At least most of the time, right?"

"I guess." He doesn't sound convinced.

I kick a bent metal bolt lying in the road. It skids across the asphalt, leaving a couple of sparks. "Know what I think about when it gets really bad?"

"What?"

"Time."

Ray gives me a puzzled look. I stop and point back down the road behind us. We can see its outline going back a couple of hundred yards, then it just dissolves into darkness.

"It's like this road. Pretend that it keeps going back forever. We can't even begin to see how far it goes. And pretend it just keeps going on ahead of us forever, too, okay?"

"Got it." Ray nods.

I hawk up a glob of spit and let it splat at my feet. "Okay, here's what I perceive. Everything on this side of my spit"—I point back down the road—"is time before I was born, when I didn't exist on Earth. And everything on *this* side of my spit"—now I point ahead—"is gonna be time after I die, when once again I won't exist here. So basically, when you look at the big picture, our lives are just a minute puddle of spit on an unimaginably long, endless road."

"But that's just what I'm saying," Ray protests. "It's so insignificant."

"Yeah, maybe. But it's the only chance we get. We already spent one forever not existing. And sooner or later we're gonna spend another forever not existing. So it seems really dumb to cut short the one little goober of time when we're actually here."

Ray looks down at the small white puddle and back at me.

"Saliva, Chase."

"Saliva, Ray."

NICOLE

It's okay." I calm Brad. "It's just me."

He presses his hand against his chest. "You almost gave me a heart attack."

We face each other across the bush. Even though Brad is quite tall, I'm resisting an intense desire to leap up and rip his eyes out.

"What are you doing here?" he asks.

"Guess."

You can almost see the lightbulb go on. "You're wondering why I asked Dulcie to the prom and not you."

"It crossed my mind."

"I'm in love." The word floats above us and spreads like the rain forest canopy, trapping every nuance and shadow while blocking out clarity.

"I'm sorry?" I know I didn't hear him right.

"I said I'm in love. With Dulcie." Brad speaks with a plain unmistakable earnestness. I almost wish he'd be nasty so that I could spray him with a fusillade of burning hot verbal lead. But instead he's honest and sincere, as if he actually understands my plight.

"With Dulcie Wheaton?" I repeat.

"I'm sorry." He bows his head.

"I don't believe that." This, for lack of anything better to say.

"I am. And I know it's really crappy to leave you without a date for the prom."

"Then can't we still go?" I ask stupidly.

Brad shakes his head. "I want to take her, Nicole. I can't do the prom with anyone else."

His words are filled with suffocating sincerity. What can I say? He loves Dulcie. He doesn't love me. He's never loved me. I'm not even sure I would have *wanted* him to love me. I just want him to take me to the prom.

"How?" The word leaves my throat in a croak.

"How did we fall in love?" Brad fills out the question. "It just happened. I guess I got tired of all this social garbage. She's so real, Nicole. There's not a phoney bone in her body. She's like a shining beacon of straightforwardness."

"And you flew to her like a moth to a flame," I finish for him.

"Something like that."

I could barf.

♛

CHASE

Wanna skate?" Ray asks.

"When?"

"Now."

"It's nearly one in the morning, Ray."

"I know a guy with an empty pool. For a six-pack, he'll let us."

"Not up for it. Sorry."

Ray's quiet for a moment. "Don't you want to skate anymore?"

That's what Dave, Ray, and I used to do. It wasn't that long ago, but somehow it feels like another lifetime.

"I don't know."

His shoulders sag. His hands are jammed back in his pockets. "No one wants to skateboard anymore. It's all cars now. I've been naturally selected out. Skating is like...kid stuff." Ray rubs his nose on the sleeve of his jacket. He seems really bummed tonight.

"You can still skate, Ray."

"With who? Little kids? Forget it. Everyone thinks I'm weird enough as it is."

"No one cares."

"Yeah, no one cares," Ray mutters. "No one cares... about me."

"Hey, man..." I put my arm around his shoulder.

Just then headlights appear. The car pulls up and stops. A girl rolls down the window and gives us a funny look. Two more girls are squeezed into the front seat with her.

I take my arm off Ray's shoulder.

"Uh, hate to interrupt." She has blond hair and a turned-up nose. Definitely cute. And she's wearing a tight, scooped-out T-shirt. Definitely hot. "There a junior high around here?"

"He said it was a middle school," pipes up one of her friends.

"Up the road, make your first right." *Is this what I think it is?*

"First right, you said?" the blonde cracks her gum.

"Yeah."

"Come on," urges her friend. "We're already late."

"Thanks." The blonde winks and the car squeals away. I watch the red taillights disappear into the dark.

Ray shakes his head slowly from side to side. "Man, if Dave ever finds out, he'll kill us."

I nod. "This has to be our little secret, Ray."

"Yeah. Dave couldn't have handled it anyway."

NICOLE

One in the morning. I'm sitting on the curb next to my driveway, crying. I know it's really stupid. Due to deforestation and erosion, 23 billion tons of tillable topsoil is being washed into the sea every year. We are probably headed for a worldwide famine that could wipe out as many as a billion people, and I have the nerve to be devastated just because I don't have a date for the prom.

Dumb...so dumb.

Why do I care? Why do I care about *any* of this? It's so infantile and superficial and yet I feel trapped by it. Everyone wants to be popular. *Everyone*. But why? What is it? Why do we want it? Why can't we just live without it?

"Nicole?"

I straighten up and wipe the tears from my eyes. Chase is standing over me in the dark. "What's wrong?"

"Nothing, I...er...was just thinking about my dad."

Chase sits down on the curb beside me. "Something happen to him?"

"Yes, no, I don't know."

"Huh?"

"I'm sorry, Chase, but I'd really like to be alone right now."

"Oh, okay." He starts to get up. That's when I realize I truly don't want to be alone. I reach up, grab his plaid shirt sleeve, and pull.

Ripppp!

"Ohmygod! Chase, I'm so sorry!" I've practically ripped the sleeve off from the elbow down.

"It's okay." He settles on the curb again. "Old shirt."

"You sure? I could sew it."

"Not worth it." He brushes his hair out of his eyes. "So what's going on? What are you doing out here, anyway?"

"Crying. What about you?"

"Just walked Ray home."

"I didn't know he needed a chaperon."

"Tonight he did."

Normally I would be more inquisitive, but I'm being totally egocentric at the moment.

"Chase, for the sake of old times, can you keep a really big secret?"

"Sure, what?"

"Would you put your arm around me?" I ask.

"Okay." He does it. "So what's the secret?"

"That I asked." I start to cry. I'm beyond caring that he knows, or that he might even tell everyone at school. But somehow I know he won't. Maybe it doesn't matter. On Monday, when everyone finds out I have no date for the prom, my house of cards is going to come crumbling down anyway.

Ripppp! Something rips again.

I look up. "What was that?"

Chase offers me the pocket from his shirt. "I don't have any tissues."

"Thanks." I blow my nose in it.

"So what's wrong?"

"It's Brad. He asked Dulcie Wheaton to the prom."

"What?" Chase takes his arm away and stares at me in the dark.

"You heard me."

"Dulcie and *Brad?*"

"Strange, isn't it?"

"I don't get it."

"Brad told me they're in love," I explain. "He says that Dulcie is a beacon of clarity in the fog of social pretense we're all lost in."

"Brad said that?"

"I know. It's like he suddenly got religion."

"Jeez."

"I mean, I can't *blame* him," I admit. "You can't blame someone for falling in love. It's just that everyone was expecting him to ask *me* to the prom. Now he's asked Dulcie and I've got no one."

I start to sob, and Chase slides his arm around my shoulders again. Truth is, in some ways he's my oldest and closest friend. We might snipe at each other, but underneath all that we have history.

"Hey, it's not that bad," he says.

"Yes it is. I know it's stupid and superficial, but I really care about things like that."

"Why?"

"Oh, please, Chase, let's not get philosophical. It's just important. To me, at least."

"Okay, you're right." He gives my shoulder a squeeze. It feels good. "How about this? If worse comes to worst, I'll take you."

CHASE

Dulcie and *Brad Selden?* I can't *believe* he asked her!

"What's taking him so long?" Dave asks. We're sitting in his car outside the Department of Motor Vehicles. Ray's inside, trying to work out some problem that's preventing him from getting his license.

"Chill, Dave." The car reeks of air fresheners because so many jocks have hurled in the back seat. The mixed scents themselves are enough to make you want to puke.

"Why do you bother with that guy?" Dave asks.

"Because he's my friend."

"A loser."

"And we're major winners?"

"I'm just saying..."

"Do me a favor? Don't."

Dave taps the steering wheel with his fingers. "I said I was sorry about the other night. I was just ticked."

Not as ticked as you'd be if you knew...

"That junk about us being the same as animals bugs me," he says.

"In some ways it's true."

"Yeah? Then how come they don't have fast food?"

I give him a look. He smiles and winks. "You hear about Brad and Dulcie? Is that bizarre or what?"

"You never know." I feign nonchalance. *And how could she say yes?*

"I mean, personally, *I've* always thought that Dulcie was seriously babe-a-licious," Dave goes on. "But she's like totally uninvolved with the social scene. And everyone thought Brad was gonna ask Nicole."

"Strange stuff." I still can't get over it. Dulcie and *Brad "Stone-Hands" Selden?* The guy's a total *GQ* boneheaded, lightweight goody-two-shoes with the intellectual depth of potting soil. Plus, he's probably the worst center in the history of high school basketball.

"Anyway, I don't know now," Dave says. "I mean, I was thinking about it. About going."

"Hmmmmm." Something that I've never quite considered before is suddenly becoming clear to me. I guess somewhere deep in my subconscious maybe I was also thinking about going to the prom…with Dulcie.

"What about you?" Dave asks.

"Huh?"

"You given the prom any thought?"

"Naw, haven't thought about it."

NICOLE

Amazingly, I get all the way to lunch on Monday without detecting a single smirk, sneer, or catty remark regarding The Great Humiliation. Clearly I've miscalculated. It almost seems as if the rest of the world doesn't care.

By lunch I've let my guard down so completely that when Alicia slides her tray beside mine at the salad bar, I don't give it a second thought.

"Are you upset?" she asks.

I blink at her uncomprehendingly for a moment, then realize what she's referring to. "Oh, well, surprised is more like it."

"It just doesn't make any sense," she goes. "I mean, did you have any inkling?"

I shake my head.

"It's a really sucky move by Brad," Alicia continues. "I mean, did he not ask Dave Ignazzi to ask me to ask you if you'd go?"

I nod.

"That's really low."

"I don't think he did it to hurt me." I play the saint. "I honestly think he's as surprised as anyone else."

Alicia wrinkles her forehead. "I don't follow. What's *he* surprised about?"

"Well, that he fell in love with Dulcie."

Alicia's eyes widen. "He's *in love* with her?"

"That's what he told me."

"*Brad* and *Dulcie?*"

"If it weren't for the fact that he's left me without a prom date, I'd probably think it was sweet."

Alicia gives me a dumbfounded look. "Are you feeling okay?"

"Well…given the circumstances."

She shakes her head wondrously. "SPURNED BY PROM DATE, GIRL LOSES MIND."

As if I have a choice?

CHASE

It's a senior privilege to go to the senior lounge at lunch instead of hanging around in the nut farm, otherwise known as the cafeteria. I find Dulcie sitting on a bench with Dave. She's laughing at something he's telling her.

"No, no, I'm serious," he's saying. "So Rope goes, 'What are you studying, Karl?' and Karl blinks and says, 'Anatomy.'"

Dulcie laughs. Dave turns to me. "Hey, Chase, you hear about Lukowsky?"

Karl Lukowsky is this goofy, nineteen-year-old perpetually left-back class pervert.

"What now?" I ask.

"He taped a *Playboy* inside the covers of a *Life* magazine and was reading it in study hall. Rope caught him, so he said he was studying anatomy."

I share the tail end of their chuckle. Then Dave gets up. "Gotta get some grub. You coming, Chase?"

"Uh, in a second."

Dave scowls, glances down at Dulcie, and back at me as if he can't figure out the connection. "Okay, see ya." He heads off.

I sit down. Dulcie studies me impassively for a moment. Suddenly I get this bad feeling. Like she's totally prepared for this. I wasn't even sure what I was going to say, but I feel like she already *knows*. Now I'm less sure.

"Did you want to talk?" she asks.

"Yeah, I guess." Still not knowing exactly what I want to say.

She smiles knowingly. "Let me guess. Does it have something to do with the prom?"

I nod, careful not to say anything bad about Brad, just in case she feels the same way about him that he does about her.

"Is it the fact that I'm going? Or the fact that I'm going with Brad?"

"Uh, maybe both."

Dulcie twirls a strand of her curly black hair around her finger. "It's funny, but I never, not for a single second, doubted that I would go to my senior prom. Even if I had to go alone."

That makes me smile.

"What's so funny?" she asks.

"It's just that you're probably the only person I know, probably the only person *in this whole school*, who actually would go to the prom alone."

"Why not?" She looks puzzled.

"You're right. There's no reason why anyone shouldn't do it, but I'm positive no one else would. It's just too gutsy. I mean, it's like saying to everyone, 'Look at me. I couldn't find anyone to go with, but I don't care, this is my prom and I'm going anyway.'"

"That's right."

I shake my head. "You've got to have serious inner strength not to care what everyone else thinks."

"So what do they think about me and Brad?" Dulcie gives me a searching look.

"Uh…let's just say it's a surprise."

"Because we're such an unlikely couple?"

"I guess."

"I like him."

That makes me wince. "Since when?"

"It's been developing for a long time…in funny little ways. A few nights ago we ran into each other at the diner and talked. I guess we both knew the time was right."

I can't believe I'm sitting here listening to this. I feel like I want to jump up and run as far away as I can. Or get totally drunk. Or find a giant eraser and just erase her from my consciousness. Like she never existed.

Dulcie studies my face. "You're upset?"

I sort of nod, sort of shrug.

"Why?"

"Jeez, Dulce, why do you think?"

She blinks. "*You* wanted to go to the prom with me?"

"I don't know." This is making me really uncomfortable.

"It never occurred to me that you'd want to go," she says.

"It's…it's more than that."

Still looking astonished, Dulcie says, "You never said anything."

"What about at your house?" I ask. "On the couch?"

"Oh…well…that's different."

Different? I don't get that at all.

NICOLE

Today's lunchtime prom-committee meeting was a solemn affair. You would have thought someone died. I suspect a lot of it's just for show and that certain other girls are secretly pleased at the news of my humiliation. But I persevered, displaying samples of invitations, and actively participating in a lively debate over the flavor of the punch.

I may be down, but I'm not out, thanks to Plan *B*.

"Nicole?" Ray Neely comes up to me in the hall while I'm heading for gym.

"Oh, hi, Ray." We were lab partners in Chemistry last year. Even though he dresses quite strangely and appears, from a distance, to be lost in space, he's actually incredibly smart. But I'm not sure we've ever said a word to each other outside of class. What could he want?

He sweeps his long, straight hair out of his face. "I, uh, just want you to know that, uh, I'd be honored if you'd accompany me to the prom."

"That's…er…sweet, Ray." Welcome to Theater of the Absurd. This can't be happening to me.

"I, uh, know that I've probably caught you by surprise," he goes on. "So I'll understand if you want to give it some thought."

He's giving me an out. It's touching, really. "Well, you're right. I'm still not sure what I want to do."

"Whatever you decide'll be okay with me."

"Thanks, Ray, it was really nice of you to ask. I really appreciate it."

"Okay, see ya." Ray disappears back into traffic. I feel like I've become a charity case.

Later, Alicia and I sit on the bleachers and watch our classmates play volleyball. I have been excused from gym because I have a blister on my little toe. Alicia's been excused because she can't find her pulse.

I've just hatched Plan *B* to her.

"You're not serious." She studies me in wonder.

"Why not?"

"Chase?"

"Yes."

"He's so…*unruly.* I can't believe he even wants to go to the prom."

"He might."

"And you'd really go with him?"

"Why not?"

"I hate to say this, but sometimes he smells."

"It's not a disregard for personal hygiene," I come to his defense. "It's his way of protesting our American obsession with cleanliness."

"Oh, now I feel *much* better." She rolls her eyes.

"Listen, he happens to be smart and charming when he feels like it. And he's not bad-looking. He's tall and has a nice build. There's a lot of potential there."

"For?"

"Turning him into a prom date to die for."

"You'd need forever."

"It's only March, my dear. With careful manipulation

I'll create him anew, mold him into the man of my dreams."

"You really think he'll go along with that?"

"If it's done subtly, he may not even realize what's happening."

Alicia shakes her head in wonder. "GIRL GIVES BIRTH TO OWN PROM DATE."

"Exactly."

CHASE

My father works weird hours. Actually, he works all the time. But sometimes I'll come home in the middle of the afternoon and he'll be there.

So I walk into the kitchen and there he is, talking on the phone.

"I've never really thought about doing it like that," he's chuckling. "Yes, of course I know that's the way most of the world does it. It just never occurred to me to do it that way."

What's he talking about?

"What's a membership cost?" he asks. I notice that he's looking across the yard at Nicole's house. Sue Maris, Nicole's mom, is in her kitchen talking on the phone and looking back at him.

"You're right," he says. "I guess if I got it by the case, I wouldn't run out so often. So listen, Chase just came in. Gotta run."

He hangs up and waves through the window at Mrs. Maris, who waves back.

"A case of what?" I take an iced tea out of the fridge.

"Toilet paper."

"Uh-oh."

"Not to worry. I picked up a roll on the way home."

"Phew." I start out of the kitchen.

"Chase?"

I stop. "Yeah?"

"Got a second?"

"About that."

He points at the kitchen table. "Have a seat."

I hesitate. "What's the subject?"

"Drugs." Dad sits. He taps his knuckles once against the table, as if still gathering his thoughts.

"Didn't we already have this talk?" I ask. "Like about eight years ago? After the sex lecture, but before the AIDS lecture."

"Maybe it's time for a review."

NICOLE

I tutor Callie three days a week at 4:30. One gets the distinct feeling that there's no Mr. Stacy around. It's not just the absence of *Sports Illustrated* in the house, it's also the framed photographs that show Stacy, Callie, or both, but with no one else. Also, every afternoon at 5:00 Dorita, Callie's baby-sitter, arrives. At quarter after five, Stacy comes into the kitchen where I'm working with Callie, gives her a kiss, and says good-bye.

I wonder where Stacy works. When she leaves, she's usually wearing a turquoise or red nylon warm-up suit and sneakers. She always carries a medium-size gym bag. From the looks of those perfectly polished fingernails, you can rule out any kind of manual labor. At the same time, she certainly doesn't dress like a secretary.

Does she waitress? She must do pretty well to live in that house and afford Dorita (Callie calls her Dorito) and me every week.

So Stacy leaves. Callie and I are doing flash cards of the six times table.

"What's your mom carry in that bag?" I ask.

"Her costume."

"Costume for what?"

"She's an actress," Callie replies brightly.

An actress? In this town?

"That's interesting, Callie. How long has your mom been an actress?"

"A long time."

This is a mystery. The community theater is currently doing *The Boys in the Band*, which has no female parts. Other than that, there's no theatrical entertainment for a hundred miles.

I want to preface this by saying that the sixties were incredibly different from the way things are now." Dad entwines his fingers, as if in prayer. "For one thing, we had Vietnam."

"I thought this was about drugs."

"We'll get there. You know we had a draft. It wasn't a voluntary Army like it is these days. A lot of guys I knew were forced to go. But it was a war many of us didn't believe in, a war halfway around the world to prevent communism from spreading into a country most of us had never even heard of."

"And nobody has communism anymore, right?" I add.

"Well, ironically, Vietnam does. But the point is, back then a lot of guys died or suffered horribly for a cause that meant nothing to us. The only people who cared about Vietnam were a bunch of politicians and generals who spent the war behind their desks in Washington. It wasn't something *they* ever had to worry about dying for."

My dad can get pretty intense sometimes. The lines around his eyes deepen and his jaw hardens and he stares at a fixed spot on the table. But usually it's about business, not something that happened thirty years ago.

I raise my hand. "Would you mind explaining what all this has to do with drugs?"

"Everything."

Briiiiiinnnnnng! The phone rings. I think I'm saved.

NICOLE

I got home and saw Chase and his father sitting in their kitchen. So I dialed his number and asked if we could talk. He sounded glad that I'd called and suggested we meet at the park at the end of our block right away.

"It's not that urgent," I said.

"See you in a second." He hung up.

We sit on the swings as the sun goes down and the clouds become pink and purple.

"Sounded like you really wanted to get out of the house," I observe.

He just nods. "So what's up?"

It's not going to be easy to do this. I have to feel him out first. I kick up my feet and start to swing. "Remember when we used to come here all the time?" I swing higher and higher. He sits and watches me.

"Yeah?"

"It's still fun." I'm swinging in long arcs now.

"I bet."

"Come on, try it."

"This is what you brought me out here for?" He pushes off and starts to swing.

"You suggested the park, remember? I just wanted to talk."

"What about?"

"I could always swing higher than you," I tease.

"Oh, yeah?"

Soon we're both swinging as high as we can. The whole swing set shakes and almost tips when we reach the tops of our arcs together.

"It's going to fall!" I cry out.

"Catch some air!" At the top of his arc, Chase launches himself out of his swing. For a split second he hangs in the twilight, silhouetted by the sunset, all arms and legs, his plaid shirt flapping. Air Chase.

"Don't!" I scream too late.

Whump! He hits the sand and crumples.

"Ohmygod!" I jam my feet against the ground, skid to a stop, and jump off. In a flash I'm kneeling on the sand, cradling his head in my lap. "Chase? *Chase!*"

His eyes are closed. He's as limp as a rag. I look around in a panic. Do I dare leave him and run to the closest house for help? Or stay here and yell? He's so still. Is he even breathing? Oh, God, what should I do?

"I can't believe you still fall for this."

Total shock. Chase is grinning up at me.

"Why, you!" I grab a handful of sand and throw it at him.

Laughing, he rolls onto his knees. "Man, some things *never* change!"

Unfortunately, he's right. He used to do the same thing when we were seven.

I always responded the same way.

By wrestling him to the ground.

"Give up?" I grunt. I'm on top, of course. Chase always let me win.

"Never!" He pushes me over and we roll around some more.

We stop abruptly. We're lying face to face in the sand, locked in an embrace, breathing hard. To a casual observer, it might resemble something other than wrestling.

CHASE

Look, I'm just going to be honest. Once the juices start flowing, we guys don't think that much about where we're going, if you catch my drift. We can always worry about that later. This is definitely the case with Nicole. I mean, you're eighteen and juiced with hormones. This fairly babe-a-licious creature is in your arms in some dark and unpopulated place, and suddenly it doesn't matter that you've practically been brother and sister all your life.

Besides, Dulcie's sort of left me in this semipermanent state of frustration.

"Chase…Chase…*CHASE!* Stop it!"

I pick up my head, all innocent. "Stop what?"

"Take your hand out of my shirt right now!"

"This hand?"

"Pig!" Nicole's teeth close on my wrist. Not enough to hurt, but enough to let me know that pain, if not amputation, is a definite possibility. I pull my hand out and sit up. Nicole tucks her shirt back in.

"So rude, Chase," she grumbles.

"Hey, *you're* the one who wanted to wrestle."

"I didn't expect you to molest me."

"I wasn't. I was just trying a new hold."

"Hardy-har-har."

"So how come we had to stop?"

Nicole makes a big deal of rolling her eyes. "For Pete's sake, Chase, why do you *think?*"

"I don't know. Seemed like we were having fun."

"Well, that's not the way I relate to you. And I'm not interested in getting pregnant."

"Not likely." I pull a foil-wrapped latex security blanket out of my wallet.

Nicole closes her eyes and grits her teeth. "Put...that ...away...Chase."

"You sure?"

"Utterly...absolutely...yes."

"Shucks."

Am I insane? First he practically rapes me, and now I'm supposed to suggest we go to the prom? He'll probably take that as an open invitation to do who knows what.

"So what did you want to talk about, anyway?" he asks.

We're sitting on the sand a safe distance apart. It's almost dark now.

"Do you remember what you said the other night when I told you Brad asked Dulcie to the prom?"

Chase scratches his head. "Uh, that I didn't have any tissues?"

"Something else." *Oh, please, Chase. Make this easier for me!*

"Uh…" He appears to be wracking his brain. "I really don't remember."

Oh, well, here goes. "You said if worse comes to worst, you'd take me."

The silence is so thick, you could snip it with cuticle scissors.

"Uhhhhh…" Chase looks down and drags his finger through the sand.

"I just want you to think about it. Would you, Chase? For old times' sake?"

He screws up his face. "Why?"

"Because."

He smirks a little. "Because now that Brad's taking Dulcie, you've got zip?"

Somehow I've managed to get through my entire high school career without putting myself into any horribly embarrassing situations. Now they've become a daily part of my existence.

Back home I give Dulcie a call. I need to know if she's really serious about Brad.

"I don't know if it's forever," she answers, "but he's different. It's interesting to be with someone who's so self-assured and always knows exactly what he's doing."

"Unlike most of us?" I ask.

"Well, the weird thing is, we're not supposed to be so self-assured at this age," she says. "I mean. the whole idea of being eighteen is that you should still be figuring things out."

"So, uh, you're saying Brad's sort of abnormal?" I ask with a smile she unfortunately can't see.

"Maybe. But I still like him."

"One last question. Does he know about us?"

Dulcie skips a beat. Her voice changes. "Nobody knows about us, Chase. Why?"

"Just wondering."

NICOLE

Chase wants to think it over.

I wonder what the New Age aromatherapy for high school is. I'd really like something that would just lift me out of all of this. A protective aura that would get me through the prom without damage to my fragile sense of self.

But after the prom, then what?

Can't think about it.

Meanwhile, there's a party at Angie Sunberg's on Saturday night. I'm invited, of course, but I'm not going. I think I know what Hester Prynne must have felt like in *The Scarlet Letter*. Only I'd wear a scarlet WPD...Without Prom Date.

Know the feeling when you discover that someone's gone through your drawers?

I wonder what Dad would say if I asked. Maybe, *"Oh, uh, I was just looking for the nail clippers."*

Right.

Rap! Rap! He knocks on the door and comes in with his Frisbee. "Want to throw?"

"No."

"Come on."

We go out to the park. My father taught me to throw the Frisbee before I was old enough to decide for myself. Back in the days when Daddy said do it, so you did it. Now I realize the only reason he taught me was because he knew someday he'd have no one else to throw with.

So we toss it around for a while. He learned all these trick throws and catches in college and he still seems to get a pretty big charge out of them. But after half an hour even he's had enough.

We sit down under a tree.

"We never finished talking about drugs," he says.

Surprise, surprise.

"One of the key phrases back in the sixties was 'The Establishment.' That meant the government. It also meant the political, social, and business leaders of the time, and the police. Basically, the people who ran the country."

Why is he telling me this stuff? What's the point?

"So The Establishment was telling us that the war in Vietnam was good, but in our hearts we knew it was bad. At the same time, The Establishment was telling us that drugs were bad."

"Let me guess. Since it was The Establishment telling you that"—I fill the rest in for him—"you figured that meant drugs were good?"

"For a large group of people under the age of thirty, drug use became a symbol of defiance. If you didn't have long hair, wear bell bottoms, and smoke pot, you were automatically suspected of being on the wrong side. The peer pressure was tremendous."

"Oh, right, and like it's different today?"

"Yes."

"Gimme a break, Dad."

NICOLE

The house has a strange new scent.

"Chamomile," explains my mother, who has assumed a lotus position on the living room floor. The faint roar of waves on a beach can be heard. No, wait, I think it's the dishwasher.

"Why?"

"It's a natural relaxant, hon." Her eyes are closed.

"Are we not relaxed?"

"We are trying."

"Let me guess, a humongous bill from the lawyers came today?"

Serene smile. "No, no, nothing like that. Something good…possibly."

"Like?"

"I'll tell you when the time is right."

♛

CHASE

In the sixties, drug use was almost a political statement," Dad's going on. "It was a way of identifying with a cause. Call them hippies, or peaceniks, or whatever. Drugs symbolized a desire for peace, a desire for a less imperialistic foreign policy. It wasn't just about getting high."

Can you believe this garbage? "But that's what they did," I remind him.

"Only with certain drugs. Using pot and acid meant you were part of this huge change in the social order. These people weren't crackheads and drug addicts."

"Sorry to interrupt, Dad, but there's something I don't get. Are you telling me this for your sake or for mine?"

"I...I just want you to understand." He's really struggling with this.

"I do understand."

"The drugs weren't as powerful back then. They weren't as addictive. There wasn't as much crime or guns. You didn't have people robbing and killing each other over pot or acid."

"Time out." I give him the hand sign. "This is really getting dumb. Know why? Because *I don't do drugs*, okay?"

Dad looks away. "There's no need to personalize—"

"Did *you* do drugs?"

He's quiet for a moment. "No, Chase, not in any significant way."

Horse waste.

Saturday night. Everyone's at Angie Sunberg's party, and I'm at home painting a poster for the prom ticket booth at school. It's been two days since I asked Chase about going. I saw him at least four times in school on Friday, and he didn't say a word. Somehow I managed to restrain myself from asking again. I will crawl just so far on these tender knees of mine.

On the other hand, I'm dying to find out. Chase doesn't have to take me if he doesn't want to. But he really should make up his mind. If he isn't going to take me, I need time to come up with another plan. Like, entering a convent.

Briiinnggg! It's the phone. Probably Alicia wanting me to come to Angie's party.

"Nicole?" I can barely hear the voice over the background bustle of a crowd and heavy thumping music. It's not Alicia.

"Who's this?" I ask.

"Stacy."

"Oh, hi, where are you?"

"It's not important. Look, I've got a super-big problem. Dorita just called. Her little boy is sick and she has to go home. I need someone to baby-sit Callie."

And just like that, I know what I want to do. I put away

the paints and go into the kitchen. Now Mom is on the phone and looking across the yard at Chase's house. In Chase's kitchen I see Rob on the phone looking back.

"I know, it's maddening," Mom is saying. "I haven't had a good night's sleep on a Friday or Saturday since she was fourteen."

"Mom?"

"Could you hold on?" Mom puts her hand over the phone. "Yes, hon?"

"I know you don't like me taking the car on Saturday nights, but this is an emergency. Callie's mom just called. She needs a baby-sitter, pronto."

Mom nods. "Go ahead."

Huh? I expected like a three-hour argument.

"Just call me later and let me know when you'll be home." Mom lifts her hand off the phone. "Nicole just got an emergency baby-sitting job.... Yes, well, when do you expect Chase?"

Half-stunned, I take the car keys and leave.

CHASE

At the mall, eating pizza.

Beep…Beep…Beep! Dave's beeper goes off.

"Angie Sunberg's," Ray and I say at the same time. We grin and slap five.

Dave looks down at the readout. "Of course."

"You don't have to go," I tell him.

"I can't let those guys drive," says Dave.

"Then let someone else drive them," I argue. "It sure beats wiping spew off your backseat."

But Dave's already getting up—a man with a mission.

Ray and I follow him out into the parking lot.

"Cars, man." Ray sounds glum. "Darwinism everywhere you look."

"What's the connection?"

"Natural selection makes you always want a little more. Do a little better, go a little faster. Because that means your genes have a better chance of getting into the next generation than the guy who doesn't do better or go faster."

"Going fast in cars tends to get us killed."

"We're animals, remember? Whatever programmed natural selection into our genes didn't know about cars or cell phones."

"And this technology thing is all about surviving better, right?" I ask. "It's supposed to make life easier and us more successful, right?"

"You got it, man. That's why you hung up your board. Faster wheels came along."

"What about you?" I ask.

"Maybe I don't want to evolve." Ray points ahead at Dave, who's opened the front door of his car and is cleaning off the front seat for whoever he's gonna chauffeur home tonight.

"I mean," says Ray, "who wants to turn into *that?*"

Angie lives in a part of town where the houses are big and have tall hedges or walls around them. You have to go through a gate to get into her driveway. As we drive up to the house, someone is out on the second-floor balcony barfing over the rail. Welcome to The Bozo Zone.

"Gives new meaning to the phrase 'April showers,'" Ray quips.

"Got an umbrella?" I ask as we get out of the car.

Angie's front door swings open and a mummy gets pushed out. His body and legs are bound by toilet paper. He'd fall down the front steps if Ray and I weren't there to catch him.

"Who's there?" a muffled voice asks from inside the cocoon.

"Chase and Ray." We help him down the steps. "Who's this?"

"Peter."

"The Rat." Dave smirks.

"Tonight, The White Rat," Ray corrects him.

Ray and I lay The White Rat down on the front lawn.

"Thanks, guys."

"No sweat."

"You guys coming or what?" Dave's waiting by the front door.

Ray sits down on the lawn. "I'll stay with The White Rat."

"Have fun." Dave and I go inside. It's the same old jock, babe, jerk-magnet scene. The place is a mess—bags of chips and cans scattered around everywhere. Music blaring, couples making out on the couches. Alex Gidden is face-down on the floor studying individual carpet fibers.

Screams and laughter filter down the stairs from the second floor.

"Who called for a ride?" Dave shouts.

More laughter and screams. Dave and I glance at each other. He makes a face like, *What a bunch of jerks.* But we both know he wishes he'd been invited.

"You want a ride, you better come!" Dave yells. "I'm not coming back."

"Yo! Just a minute!" a voice calls down.

Dave crosses his arms like he's annoyed about having to wait.

On the second floor, a door swings open. Brad Selden backs out and waves back into the room. "Later, everyone!"

A split second later Dulcie comes out of the room with a big grin on her face.

Our eyes lock.

Her grin fades.

I turn around and head outside.

NICOLE

There must be something wrong with me.

I'm seventeen years old. Why am I happier watching *The Lion King* with a nine-year-old than going out and partying?

"Do you like Rafiki?" Callie asks. We're sitting on a bunch of throw pillows in the den, eating microwave popcorn. She's wearing purple pajamas with red dots.

"He's okay."

"He scares me." Callie yawns.

"Uh-oh, your mom didn't tell me your bedtime."

"Uh, eleven-thirty."

"Yeah, right, wise guy." I can't help smiling.

After Callie washes, I go into her room to tuck her in.

"Oh, wow!" I've never been in her bedroom before. It's every little girl's fantasy, filled with stuffed animals, dolls, a huge doll house, and a big brass bed with lots of pillows and a frilly white-laced bedcover. When it comes to her daughter, it's pretty obvious that Stacy spares no expense.

"Dorito always stays till I fall asleep," Callie says in that squeaky cute-little-girl voice.

I give her a look.

"It's true!" she insists.

"Okay, move over."

Callie slides over and I sit down next to her.

"Do you and Dorito talk?" I ask.

"Not much."

"You just like her to be close while you fall asleep?"

"Uh-huh."

I sit in the dark. Callie keeps fidgeting under the covers.

"Can't sleep?" I ask.

"Unh, unh."

"Something wrong?"

"What's your daddy like?" she asks.

"He's nice, but sad."

"Why?"

"I don't know, Callie. He won't tell me."

She's quiet for a second. "I wonder if my daddy's sad, too."

"When was the last time you saw him?"

"I never have."

"You've *never* seen your father?"

"Mommy says I saw him when I was a baby. But I don't remember."

"What happened?"

"Mommy told him to go away."

"Why?"

"I don't know. How come some dads go away and others don't?"

"Good question."

"Why did your daddy go away?" she asks.

"Uh, he and my mom didn't get along anymore."

"Do you miss him?"

"Sort of. But I get to see him every week. Do you miss your dad?"

"I wish he'd tuck me in at night."

I feel like crying.

CHASE

Of all the...

I step through the front door and out into the night. The White Rat is still wrapped in toilet paper, lying on the lawn like a big white grub. Ray is lying on the ground next to him.

"Does he need help?" I ask.

"Naw, he's cool," Ray says.

"He's just gonna lie there all night?"

"It's pretty comfortable," says The White Rat.

"You'll freeze."

"I can get out if I want." The White Rat starts wriggling and squirming around. Doesn't look like he's getting very far.

"Hey, Chase, how about it?" Dave is getting into the car. Brad is holding the back door for Dulcie. I look down at Ray.

"You coming?" I ask.

He shakes his head.

"You won't leave The Rat like that, right?"

"When he comes out, he's gonna be a butterfly," Ray replies.

I get in the front seat with Dave and try not to look at Dulcie and Brad in the back. I know his arm's around her, and they're huddled comfortably in the corner.

"Where to?" Dave asks when we get to the end of the driveway.

"My house?" Brad directs the question at Dulcie. "My parents aren't home."

I can feel the hair on the back of my neck rise. *Why didn't I stay behind with Ray? Why did I have to come along for this?*

"I guess," Dulcie replies halfheartedly.

"*Jesus H. Christ,*" I can't help muttering.

"Huh?" Brad grunts.

"Nothing."

Dave doesn't ask directions to Brad's. Guess he knows the way by heart. I hear rustling in the backseat.

"Stop it, Brad," Dulcie hisses.

"What's wrong?" Brad whispers.

There's a whisking sound as Dulcie slides across the seat to the other corner.

Then silence.

"Good party?" Dave asks.

"Yeah, pretty good," Brad grumbles, a hint of annoyance in his voice.

"What do you think of Indiana's chances?"

"What?"

"In the NCAAs," Dave says.

"Gee, I don't know, Dave. What do *you* think?" Brad's voice drips with sarcasm. Like he could give a crap.

"I think they've got a real shot," Dave says. Can't he see them laughing at him? How can he be so thick?

"Say, Dave, you going to the prom?" Brad asks.

"Uh, not sure. Why?"

"Me and my friends have been pricing limos," Brad

says. "They're a fortune. Maybe we could rent something really nice for you to drive."

What a sport!

"Uh, I'll have to think about it." Dave clings to some last shriveled shred of self-respect.

Silence.

We turn onto a street with small houses nestled tightly together, and pull into a driveway. Brad unfolds out and holds the door for Dulcie. I look back over the seat and lock eyes with her.

"Well?" Brad asks. Standing outside the car, he can't see the look Dulcie and I are sharing.

"I think I'll go home," Dulcie says.

"What?" Brad bends down and sticks his head in. I turn around and pretend to mind my own business. "But you said—"

"I've got a headache," Dulcie replies.

"You didn't have one a minute ago," says Brad.

"Well, she's got one *now*, okay?" I blurt.

"Chase!" Dulcie's voice is filled with chastisement.

Dave stares at me in shock, like I've just broken some ancient taboo against raising one's voice to a *GQ* jock-brained, robo-geek.

"What's *that* all about?" Brad asks Dulcie.

"Nothing," Dulcie says quickly. "I'll call you tomorrow, okay?"

"Yeah, sure." Brad's reply is etched with disappointment.

I hide a smile. *Tough luck, dipwad.*

A few minutes later we pull up to the curb in front of Dulcie's house. Once again, I look over the seat at her.

I have to get Brad to invite me to the prom

You'd think Alicia and I were good friends

My next-door neighbor, Chase

My dream is on the verge of coming true

They clean up pretty nicely!

Summer fun

The prom—oh, and Brad and Alicia

♥ ♥ ♥ *Who knew?* ♥ ♥ ♥

"Thanks for the ride, Dave." Her face is expressionless.

I hop out and open the door for her.

"See you later?" I whisper as she gets out.

Dulcie stares at me in the dark. Then her eyes dart down toward Dave, in the front seat. Without a word she goes up the path to her house.

I watch her for a moment, then get back into the car.

"Where to?" Dave asks.

"The Milky Way."

He drives a couple of blocks, then I tell him to stop.

"Huh? Why?"

"Don't know." I push open the door and get out. "Just feel like walking, I guess."

"You serious?" Dave asks. "It's one o'clock in the morning and you're a mile away from home."

"Yeah." I'm aware of that.

NICOLE

"Nicole?"

I open my eyes and quickly sit up. For a moment I don't know where I am. Stacy's big-hair silhouette is backlit in the bedroom doorway. Now I remember.

"Oh, hi." I stretch and get off Callie's bed.

"Everything go okay tonight?" Stacy steps quietly into the room.

"Oh, yeah, she's a doll. What time is it?"

"A little after one. Sorry I'm late. Busy night." We pass each other as I head for the living room and Stacy heads for Callie. The strong, tart odor of cigarette smoke wafts along with her.

I wander into the living room, squinting in the light. Stacy's gym bag is on the coffee table. *Busy night?* When she called before, it sounded like she was at a party.

Stacy comes back out. "What did she have for dinner?"

I tell her.

"And she brushed her teeth?"

"As far as I know. Think I could use your phone? I promised my mom I'd call when I was leaving."

"Sure. Use the one in the kitchen."

In the kitchen I dial home. Meanwhile, I can still see into the living room. Stacy unzips the gym bag and starts to rummage through the contents.

"Hello?"

"Hi, Mom, sorry to call so late. Stacy just got in. I'm coming home."

"Okay, hon. See you soon."

She hangs up. Funny, she's usually asleep by eleven o'clock, but just now she sounded wide awake. I hang up and look back into the living room. Stacy's still groping around in the gym bag for her wallet. To make it easier, she pulls out several items and places them on the table beside her...a pair of spiky black high heels, and a frilly white garment that definitely qualifies as lingerie. *Busy night?* What, exactly, does she do?

"She wants me to come right home," I call from the kitchen, moving slowly and giving Stacy time to repack the items, which she quickly does.

She has a funny look on her face when she pays me. "Hope you don't mind fives and ones." She hands me a small wad of bills. Oddly, almost all of them are creased lengthwise down the middle.

"I'll take it any way I can get it."

A smile works through her lips. "A girl after my own heart."

♛

CHASE

Dulcie's house is a ranch, so everyone sleeps on the ground floor. The windows of her bedroom start just above eye level. The light's on. I tap my finger gently against the glass. The curtain parts, and Dulcie's face appears. She slides the window open.

"Hi." She smiles.

"I was just walking by and noticed the light was on."

Her smile broadens. "You can't come in, and my parents will hear me if I come out."

"This is okay. How come you changed your mind about going to Brad's?"

"I don't know, I just did."

"Didn't have anything to do with me being in the front seat, did it?"

"Don't get too full of yourself, Chase." But she winks.

"I still don't get what you see in him."

Dulcie reaches out the window and strokes my hair with her fingers. "You're so in the dark."

"Then enlighten me."

She sighs. "Boys have sports, Chase."

"Huh?"

"That's where you compete. That's where you get to prove who's the strongest or fastest or most coordinated. It's very up front and obvious to everyone."

"So?"

"Girls have a different playing field."

"They have sports, too," I point out.

"It's not the same thing."

"What about school?" I ask.

"You can be a brain and still be a loser. Look at Sandy Kimmel."

I stare at her in wonder. "I can't believe I'm hearing this from *you* of all people. I mean, if there was ever someone who didn't care about all that social garbage."

"That's where you're wrong," she says. "I'm just what you'd call a holdout."

"A guy who won't play until he gets the money he wants?"

Dulcie nods.

"I don't see the connection."

She leans out the window and kisses me on the forehead. "Think about it, Chase. I'm going to bed."

Walking home at 2:00 A.M. The moon is full tonight, a big bright orb in the sky. I can't believe it. *I just can't believe it!* Dulcie always pretended not to care about the social garbage. But all this time she did! She just refused to show it until she got what she wanted—Brad Selden.

Walking up my street, every house is dark at this hour. There's Nicole's house. Poor Nicole...the girl who was *supposed* to go to the prom with Brad.

Hey! That gives me an idea.

NICOLE

Monday morning at Time Zone. Chase and I are walking along slowly. Kids jostle us front and back. Chase always walks with his hands in his pockets, so I slide my arm through his. It's not a romantic thing; just a way to keep us from getting separated by the mob.

"Listen." I speak in a low voice. "About what I said the other day."

"Yeah, I was gonna get back to you on that," he replies. "I—"

"It's okay," I cut him short. "It was a moment of weakness. I mean, you probably weren't planning to go and—"

Chase stiffens. We've come face-to-face with Brad and Dulcie. *And his arm is around her shoulder!*

Chase starts to pull his arm away from mine, but I squeeze down on it as hard as I can while forcing a smile on my face. Dulcie looks puzzled. Brad's face is a mask.

No one says a thing.

The human current sweeps us past each other. I let Chase remove his arm from mine.

"Nice move," he mutters.

"Sorry, it was a reflex."

"You know, it's not a *competition*." Chase's voice is caustic. "It's not, 'You've got a girlfriend so I have to have a boyfriend.' There's supposed to be some kind of *basis* for a relationship."

"Yes, Dr. Hammond."

We grin at each other.

"So, about the prom," I remind him.

"Let's do it," he says.

Huh? I stop in the middle of the hall and stare at him.

"What?" He looks confused. "Hey, it's only the prom."

Pollution is no longer limited to certain geographic areas, such as around steel mills or chemical plants. It is now everywhere. It is no longer just a problem of industrialized nations. Some of the worst polluters are the unregulated developing countries. Unless something is done to slow pollution down, there will be no high school proms in the year 2200.

But there'll be one this year, *and I'm going!*

♛

CHASE

Nicole and I walk home together after school. It's a reasonably warm, sunny afternoon. Little green buds have started to sprout from the tree branches. Looks like the grim, gray veil of winter has begun to lift.

"Are you *sure?*" she asks.

"Why not?"

"I just want to make sure," she says. "There's a lot of preparation, you know."

"Like what? We're going."

"It's not just about *going* to the prom. It's *how* you go."

"Huh?"

Nicole gives me this very serious look. "Listen carefully, Chase. Once the word gets out that you and I are going to the prom, do you know what people are going to think? 'Oh, sure, Nicole couldn't get Brad to take her, so she got her old friend Chase to take her.'"

"So? Who cares?"

"Chase, why are you going to the prom?"

"Well…" I can't tell her about Dulcie. "It'll be a scam."

"If you really want it to be a scam, don't do it half-heartedly. Go all the way. Make it a *real* scam. We don't want to slink in there looking like two dorks who couldn't find anyone else to go with. We want to make it look like our going to the prom is the ultimate result of an incredible whirlwind romance that took us totally by surprise. We want to make it look like it's the logical and final step, Chase. Like *we have no choice* but to go."

My first reaction is that it's totally phoney. I'm not going to *pose*. But then…it's weird. In a way, that's exactly how Dulcie set it up. Except in her case, Brad's too thick to see it.

"So what do we do?" I ask.

"We…fall in love."

NICOLE

Time is of the essence. There's so much to accomplish.

"Where were you Saturday night?" Alicia asks as we walk toward the weekly PPC meeting.

"Busy." I feign preoccupation with thought.

Alicia scowls. "Don't tell me you totally forgot about Angie's party."

"Ohmygod!" I gasp.

Alicia studies me. "Wow, you must have *really* been busy. Want to tell me about it?"

I shake my head.

"Why not?"

"It's too soon."

"*Alleeeeeeeeeeeeeeeesha!*" The shrill scream pierces our eardrums. Everyone in the hall stops and looks around.

"*Who's doing that?*" Alicia wails.

But the screamer is nowhere to be found. A moment later we're back in the orderly flow of bodies on their way to another educational experience. Alicia and I duck into a room and join the other members of the prom committee.

The meeting proceeds smoothly. A band has been chosen, decorations and punch flavors agreed upon, an official prom photographer selected. Then Sandy Kimmel raises her hand.

"Yes, Sandy?" I call on her.

"I'd really like to resolve the Grand March thing," she says. "Can't we just get rid of it?"

Hardly a meeting goes by that Sandy doesn't raise this issue. Now that I'm going with Chase, we're a probable Top-Twelve couple, but it's going to take a miracle to break into the Final Four. Meanwhile, Brad and Dulcie are practically assured of a Final-Four spot, if simply by default. I look around the room, knowing that Chloe doesn't particularly care and that Alicia, who may or may not be going with Jason, is only Top Twelve at best.

Should I care?

No.

But I do.

"It doesn't make a big difference to me, Sandy," I answer. "But I do feel a responsibility toward future proms. I mean, do we have the right to abolish a tradition that's been going on for forty years?"

"If a future prom committee feels strongly about the Grand March, they can always reinstate it," Sandy cleverly replies.

Uh-oh... I give Alicia a desperate look. *Help!*

"Well, Sandy," Alicia begins, "I really think you may be taking a narrow approach to this. The Grand March isn't just about us. It's about our parents and families, too. I mean, isn't that why they all went out and spent a fortune on video cameras?"

Sandy blinks, but does not respond.

Saved by Alicia!

CHASE

I'm in Deep Cable, Channel 68. Three former semiobscure professional athletes, *and their dogs*, are competing against each other in the man–dog relay race.

Is it my imagination, or has TV gotten truly pathetic?

Thoughts begin to drift…to the prom. Like I said before, Nicole is fairly babe-a-licious, and I've pretty much always liked her when I haven't hated her. I have no problem with making everyone believe we're in love…except for Dulcie.

On the other hand, Dulcie doesn't seem to care how I feel about her and Brad.

So why not? Dulcie says she's been holding out all this time.

Guess what? So have I.

The prom…what a goof. Maybe I'll wear a sky-blue tux with a pink frilly shirt.

The former semiobscure professional athletes and their dogs are now competing in the Frisbee toss. My father ought to be there.

Lame…eyes drift up to the bookshelf. There's Dad's high school yearbook. Take a look? It can't be worse than the man–dog high jump.

The book has that old attic smell. The binding cracks as I open it. Hmmm…ever look at your parents' high school yearbooks? There's this delayed-reaction thing inside. Like all that psychedelic flower child stuff from the late sixties didn't filter down into yearbooks until the seventies. So all the senior girls have long straight hair parted in the middle, and all the guys have sideburns and floppy long hair. But they're still trying to comb it in the old styles. Strange stuff.

Hey, wait a minute! What's this? A picture of Chester Potts in my old man's yearbook! Except, he's not a janitor here, he's a senior!

I carry the book into my father's office. That is, his office here at home so he can still work when he's not at work. It's a single-parent, workaholic thing: "I need to spend time with my child, so I'll work at home and ignore him."

"Yo, Dad."

He looks up from his computer. "Hey, Chase."

"I didn't know you were in the same class as Chester Potts." I lay the yearbook on his desk, open to Chester's picture. "He's a janitor at Time Zone."

"Chester Potts..." Dad presses his hands together and gazes up at the ceiling.

"You remember him?"

Dad hesitates. "Uh...vaguely."

"Weird dude, huh?"

"I don't recall."

NICOLE

Scientists estimate that one hundred years ago, more than 200,000 blue whales lived in the oceans. Today, less than 2,000 survive. The Atlantic gray whale has vanished altogether. Overfishing is devastating many populations of fish and mollusks. Coral reefs are being destroyed at a hellish rate.

Why can't we stop wrecking the world?

Why won't Chase stay still?

"I can't believe I'm letting you do this." He's squirming like a five-year-old.

"Stop being such a baby," I scold him.

I'm cutting his hair in my kitchen. Chase is sitting in a chair with a towel draped over his shoulders.

"My hair!" he cries, as a large clump tumbles to the floor.

"Believe me, Chase, this will be the greatest joke you've ever played."

"But no one will know it."

"We'll tell everyone at our tenth reunion."

"Nicky?" Mom pokes her head into the kitchen. She's got a laundry basket under her arm. "Can I speak to you for a moment?"

I pat Chase on the head. "Don't go anywhere, handsome." Then I go out into the hall.

"Whose clothes are these?" Mom whispers, gesturing to the laundry basket, which is full of jeans, T-shirts, and plaid shirts.

"Chase's," I whisper back.

"Why are they in our wash?"

"You're so good at doing stuff like that," I whisper. "And Chase and his dad are like, incompetent at laundry."

It's an utterly lame explanation, but the best I can manage at the moment. I expect Mom to inform me that if I want Chase's laundry done, I'll have to do it myself.

Instead, she just sighs and heads for the laundry room.

♛

CHASE

Playing Terminator Two at the mall. It's hard to find this game anymore, which is unfortunate because it's one of the best. Ray and I are lucky the arcade still has one. Sometimes you can even find one with the fake recoil action still working, but that's really rare.

Blam! Blam! Blam! We're mowing down Terminators, blasting lights, having a ball. Very satisfying.

"Explain video games in terms of natural selection," I challenge him.

"Whoa, tough one." Ray doesn't take his eyes off the targets. "Okay. Like part of the genetic code programs us for aggression—survival by beating our competitors."

"Attila and the boys?"

"Exactly. So we're living up to our genetic code in a way that society finds 'acceptable.' Just like sports, and probably why guys find playing touch football with girls so weird. We're only programmed to compete against other guys."

"Are we better or worse than people who don't play video games?" I ask.

"Another hard call. Everyone has to work off their aggression. People put down video violence, but it sure beats what my old man used to do."

"Which was?"

"Come home and beat on us every night."

"What happened?"

"One night he beat my mom up pretty bad. Now he goes to Beaters Anonymous."

"Cuffs?" someone says behind us.

We turn around and find Dave looking down at the new pair of slacks Nicole convinced me to buy.

Now Ray's staring at them, too. "Mr. Bogus, man."

"And what happened to your hair?" Dave wants to know.

"Don't ask."

NICOLE

I smile up at Chase, my eyes aglow with love and affection.

"This is ridiculous." He's squirming again.

"I'm starting to think that's your mantra."

"I can't believe I let you talk me into buying pants with *cuffs!*"

"If you really hate them, I can do alterations."

"I don't know about this, Nicole."

"Say anything you want," I coo. "Just keep smiling at me."

We're facing each other, and leaning against the wall opposite the auditorium. The whole high school is filing past us and into the auditorium for an assembly by some writer (Snore!). Chase turns to look at them.

"Don't look," I whisper sweetly. "You want to appear utterly and totally entranced by me, as if nothing else in the world matters."

"This is so fake," he grumbles through clenched teeth. "And what's with keeping my shirt tucked in all the time?"

"Love has made you clean up your act."

Chase grimaces.

"Come on, you're doing great," I whisper. "And I like your haircut."

"You *ought* to."

"Ha!" I burst out in peels of appreciative laughter.

"It wasn't *that* funny," Chase growls through his concrete smile.

"I know." I smile back.

"I can't believe this." He shakes his head. The smile is starting to crumble.

"Chuckle," I whisper.

"Huh?"

"I said, chuckle."

"Jeez, Nicole." But he does chuckle.

"They're almost all inside. Just a minute or two more."

"And then?"

"We can go in."

"And?"

"Sit together in the back away from everyone else."

"You have this whole thing worked out."

"Image is everything," I remind him.

"That's old."

"Doesn't mean it isn't true."

CHASE

Why'd you do it?" Dulcie looks up at my hair with a puzzled expression. We've just run into each other in the hall.

"Time for a change." I shrug.

"But it's not you."

"Hey, who knows who I am?"

"I do."

I'd like to ask her how she can always be so sure of herself. What does she know that I don't?

"Don't let Nicole change you," she says.

"Who said anything about Nicole?"

Dulcie gives me a knowing look and walks away.

I turn around and come face-to-face with Mr. Rope.

"Chase?" He looks surprised.

"Yeah?"

"You look different…cleaned up."

I quickly look around. "Not so loud, Mr. Rope. Someone might hear you."

He gives me a wry look. "You haven't been in my office for nearly three weeks. Something wrong?"

"Guess I've been busy."

"*Alleeeeeeeeeeeeeeeesha!*" The scream hurtles down the hallway, making me wince. Sounds like the cry of a total madman.

Mr. Rope narrows his eyes. "Excuse me, Chase. I've got to find the person responsible for that."

Alicia's in my bedroom. We're trying on things to wear for tonight.

"I don't believe you," she says, standing in front of the mirror, holding a semi-see-through top against herself. "And I *can't* believe him."

"Why not?"

"He's a Stud Muffin."

"Told you so." I smile proudly.

"I mean, he's not a Brad Selden, but still. GRUNGE BOY TRANSFORMED INTO FROG PRINCE."

"This isn't about comparisons," I remind her.

"What about the body odor thing?"

"I told you before. He's not hygienically impaired. He just saw it as a protest statement."

"But it's under control?"

"I believe so."

"Then you've done it," she says wondrously.

"Done what?" Time to play dumb.

"You got Chase to take you to the prom."

I let my jaw drop with suitable implications of surprise.

"What's wrong?" Alicia asks.

"I totally forgot about that!" I gasp.

"What do you mean?"

"I mean, we haven't even talked about the prom." *Liar, liar, pants on fire.*

The lines in Alicia's forehead deepen. "Then what's this all about?"

I raise my hands in a helpless gesture. "I honestly don't know. It's just something that happened."

CHASE

Party time.

In the bathroom mirror, my hair is short and neat, my shirt pressed and tucked in. Jeez, I look like a geek. What am I doing to myself?

My father's sitting on the living room couch, reading through computer printouts. He looks up. "Hot date?"

"Not really."

"You just want to look your best for Ray?"

"Yuck, yuck."

"Seriously, Chase."

"I'm going out, okay?"

"Like that?"

"It's a costume party. I'm a shock-therapy victim."

"Touché."

Just then I remember I had pizza with a lot of garlic at lunch. "We have any Tic Tacs?"

"Drawer under the microwave."

I go into the kitchen. Inside the drawer is a Ziploc bag with half a dozen packs of Tic Tacs inside. In another Ziploc bag are all the wire twists that used to float freely around the bottoms of all the drawers. Yet another bag is filled with our collection of refrigerator magnets.

Guess Dad's getting organized in his old age.

A moment later I'm heading back through the living room again.

131

"When do you think you'll be back?" Dad asks.

"Whenever."

"Seriously, Chase, I need to know."

"Eleven the earliest, two the latest."

Dad nods. "No rush."

Huh?

NICOLE

It's our "coming-out." We're going to the movies with Eddie Lampel and Bo Vine (who has changed her name to Delia and wants everyone to call her Dee Vine), and Jason and Alicia.

Chase comes over and we wait together. He sits on the edge of the couch with his hands pressed together in his lap.

"Don't be nervous," I tell him.

"Who's nervous?" he shoots back.

"Sorry."

He stands up and starts to pace with his hands in his pockets. It still shocks me to see how well he's turned out. Either I'm a miracle worker, or he's even better-looking than I thought.

"This is really dumb."

"It's just a movie."

"I've never said two words to these people."

"Then it's a good time to start."

He glares at me.

"They're just people, Chase. Human beings like you and me. They're not going to bite your head off."

"You two haven't left yet?" Mom comes into the room while putting on an earring. She's wearing a flower-print dress and makeup.

"They'll be here any second," I answer. "Where are *you* going?"

"Out."

"On a date?"

"No, just getting together with a friend." She's being more than slightly evasive.

Honk! Honk! That must be Alicia. I'll have to grill my mother later.

So we get into the car and everyone's acting friendly. The girls do most of the talking on the way to the movie. Now and then the guys grunt. We park, get tickets, go in. No big deal.

After the movie we go to the diner, where once again the girls do almost all the talking. The guys eat and grunt. Then Nicole and Alicia get up to use the bathroom, and Eddie and Jason go over to the jukebox to pick some tunes.

I'm left sitting across from Bo, I mean, Dee Vine, to whom I've probably said three words in my entire life.

"How's it going?" she asks.

"Okay." Shrug. "You?"

"Okay. You got a haircut."

"Yeah, the new me." I grin.

"I like it."

"Thanks."

She smiles. "Isn't it weird?"

"What?"

"How you can change?"

I start to think back and remember that last year, and all the years before that, Bo, I mean, Dee, was this sort of smart, fat, quiet girl with mousy brown hair. Now she's babe-a-licious with wavy reddish-brown hair and makeup. Come to think of it, she changed her name at the same time.

"It's just the outside," I whisper, feeling like we're sharing a little secret.

"Sometimes changing the outside affects the inside," she says. "I'm still me, but different, too."

Is this like, a Prozac moment?

We grin at each other.

NICOLE

It's late and we're home again. Chase walks me to my front door.

"Was *that* so bad?" I ask.

He shakes his head. "I didn't do anything. I hardly said two words."

"Not true. You listened. You laughed when someone said something funny. You didn't try to dominate the conversation, and you weren't obnoxious."

"That's all there is to it?" He seems bewildered.

"Most of the time."

"I always thought there was some magic. Something that separated the ins from the outs."

"Fear and looks."

"Huh?"

"The ins always want to look good," I explain. "They're terrified by anything, or anyone who might make them look bad. So if you make them look good, you're in."

"What if you're not particularly good-looking yourself?"

"Then you better have a fabulous wit or a lot of money."

"Bogus."

"Maybe, but I see a great future for you," I tell him. "Frankly, the ins are all bored with each other. They've basically had the same clique since fourth grade. Now you come along, and you're different and new, but you've shown that you're willing to follow the rules—"

"You mean, not embarrass anyone or make them look bad?"

"Exactly. You're the new flavor, Chase."

Chase smiles. In the dim light and shadows he looks handsome. And despite what he said, he really was charming and at ease tonight, once again exceeding my expectations.

Now it's late and our date is coming to an end, and I suddenly realize I don't want it to. I want it to keep going. But, if it really has to end, at least he could take me in his arms and kiss me.

Huh?

CHASE

Late. The house is dark. Dad must be sleeping. I've just come from the diner, but all of a sudden I'm famished. Like the nervous knot that's been in my stomach all night has finally disappeared.

I flick on the kitchen light and pull open the refrigerator.

Suddenly I hear the kitchen door open behind me.

"Wha…" I whirl around, not knowing what to expect. But it's just Dad coming in from the backyard.

At 1:00 A.M.?

He's wearing a brown crew-neck sweater and cords. His hair's a little tousled, and there's this reddish tint around his mouth.

"Where have *you* been?" I ask.

"Out."

"No kidding. Why'd you come in the back?"

"Just getting some air."

"What's the red stuff around your mouth?"

He pulls a handkerchief out of his back pocket, wipes his mouth, and looks at it. "That's funny," he says with a frown. Then he forces what seems to be a phoney yawn. "I'm bushed. Guess I'll hit the sack."

He leaves the kitchen. I find half a pint of Häagen-Dazs Chocolate Chocolate Chip and settle down to finish it off. Funny thing about tonight. It wasn't so bad. Nicole's not that different when she's with her crowd, just a little more *on*. I was worried she might get cool or snotty, but she was warm and friendly. I liked being with her.

But...

This is getting confusing. Like where does the *scam* end and the real stuff begin?

NICOLE

Sunday with Daddy. We go to the art museum (Yawn!), but at least it's free. Dad's car is small, old, and dented. It squeaks loudly and the upholstery is torn.

"Time for a new car, Dad."

"Oh?" he smiles. "Your treat?"

"How about leasing?" (I'm so financially sophisticated!)

Dad gives me a surprised look.

"They're always advertising in the newspapers," I explain.

"Can't afford it, hon."

"Because every penny you've got is going to lawyers?"

"More or less."

"There's something I don't get. If Mom's spending all *her* money on lawyers, and you're spending all *your* money on them, why don't you just bag the lawyers and work it out by yourselves?"

"We can't."

"Why not?"

"Too many things we can't agree on. I can only give so much, but she wants more. So the lawyers have to battle it out."

I let out a big wistful sigh. "I wish it was over already."

"I know." He sighs, too. "It's horribly unfair to you. I'm truly sorry."

"But you won't reconcile with Mom?"

"It's way beyond that."

"When do I find out what's going on? When I'm sixty?"

He smiles crookedly. "Before that."

The art museum happens to be located on the campus of the nearby state college I will attend next year while continuing to live at home. I could have gotten into a much better private college, but we don't have the money for that kind of tuition, room and board.

(Another way to look at it is, we *did* have the money, but now it's going to send some lawyer's kid to private college. Oh, please don't assume I'm the least bit bitter.)

Inside, we stroll along the halls lined with paintings. The artists on display are a mixture of major unknowns, the seriously obscure, and some local talent (especially if they contribute to the museum fund).

"Uh, Dad, the toupee's crooked."

"Thanks." He stops and straightens it in the reflection of a glass-covered painting.

"By the way, thanks for getting me the tutoring job."

"Oh, is it working out?" We start walking again.

"So far so good. There's just one thing I don't understand. How do you know Stacy? How'd you know her daughter needed tutoring?"

"She's a friend of a friend."

The art museum has a little sculpture garden in a courtyard with some benches, and trees growing out of big wooden pots. The sculptures are mostly fat, naked bronze women or wild animals made out of rusting car parts.

Dad and I sit on a bench. The April sun is shining. It feels good after the long, gloomy winter.

Dad squeezes my hand. "I miss you."

"I miss you, too, Dad."

A blackbird lands on a bronze lady's head and cocks its yellow eye curiously at us.

"Why don't you come home?" I ask for the seven hundredth time.

Dad stares down at the cobblestones. "I can't."

"Dad, I know you can't tell me what's going on, but can you at least tell me if you're happy?"

He takes a deep breath and lets it out slowly. "Every now and then, for a few moments, I am deliriously happy. Happier than I've been in a very long time. The rest of the time I'm fairly miserable."

"Is it worth it?"

"I guess. It almost doesn't matter, Nicky."

"Why?"

He just shrugs.

I really don't get this.

♛

CHASE

Lunch sucks. I could use a slice of Jeff Branco's boys' room pizza, but I'm broke. Ray owes me money. He swore he'd pay me.

"You seen Ray?" I ask Designated Dave.

He shakes his head. I look around the lunchroom and spy Lukowsky sucking on a packet of catsup. "Hey, Lukowsky, you seen Ray?"

"Yeah, going out to the garage."

"You sure?" That doesn't sound like Ray. The stoners gather each day behind the garage to smoke.

"Where're you going?" Dave asks.

"He owes me money."

Dave chuckles. "This I have to see."

Out behind the garage, the stoners are lighting up. Am I seeing things? Ray gives us a goofy grin and offers a blunt to Dave. "Purple hair, man. Try some?"

"Get that thing away from me, dirtbag." Dave makes a fist.

Ray offers the blunt to me.

"Since when?" I ask.

"Whenever." Ray shrugs.

Dave snorts. "Here's a new low."

"It's a free country."

"Getting lit in the middle of school?" Dave shakes his head in disgust.

"I find this hard to comprehend, Ray," I add.

"Hey, leave all judgments at the door."

So I sigh. "You wouldn't happen to have any of the money you owe me, would you?"

"Aw, man." Ray puts on this pained look. "I did this morning, but…" He points at the blunt.

"What a surprise!" Dave gasps facetiously.

"You spent *all* your money?" I ask.

"Good drugs are expensive, man."

"This is truly demented. Come on, Chase, let's bail." Dave starts to pull me back toward the cafeteria, but I hesitate and give Ray a seriously skeptical look.

He answers by taking another hit. "Big day today."

"New shipment coming in?" Dave guesses sardonically.

"No, man, my driver's test."

"You're gonna take your driver's test stoned?" I ask incredulously.

"It relaxes me," Ray explains.

"Did it ever occur to that vegified brain of yours that maybe you should leave the world safe for the rest of us?" Dave asks.

"I'm gonna be safe," Ray insists. "You'll never see *me* drink and drive."

♛

NICOLE

What's this about you and Chase?" Mom asks. We're in the car, going to the printer to pick up the invitations for the prom.

"I don't know."

She gives me a knowing look. "That's not what I hear."

"What do you hear?"

"You're an item."

"Maybe." Can I tell her? Can I trust my own mother not to divulge our little scam? Wait a minute. If it's a scam, why do I keep daydreaming about kissing him?

"I'm not so sure it's a good idea, Nicole."

What? My mother has never interfered with my relationships before. Wait, what am I thinking? It *isn't* a relationship. But…

"Why not, Mom?"

"Well…er…for one thing, you're neighbors. For another, you've been friends for a long time. You're practically brother and sister."

"So?"

"So if it goes sour, it could ruin a good friendship," she says. "Relationships come and go, Nicky, but friendships should be preserved."

"Don't worry about it, Mom." But I can't help biting my lip. *What if she's right?*

CHASE

I've been invited to a jock party. First time ever. Alex Gidden's house. Amazing.

So I'm sitting in our kitchen reading the paper, killing time till it's time to go.

Dad comes in and pulls open the fridge. He's whistling to himself. "Hey, Chase, whatsup?"

"Nothing."

"Did I hear something about your clothes showing up in the Marises' laundry?"

"Nicole's giving me a makeover."

He pulls out some ice water and goes over to the counter for a glass. "So that explains the hair."

"Yeah."

"Something brewing between you two?"

"Nah, she just needs a date for the prom. I'm doing her a favor." *But if I'm just doing her a favor, how come I can't wait to see her tonight?*

"I see. But isn't the prom still some time away?"

"Less than two months. There's prep work involved."

Dad sits down at the table and takes a sip of his water. "Seen Chester Potts lately?"

"Just about every day, why?"

"He was one of the last to go over."

"Huh?"

147

"Vietnam. Got the Purple Heart."

"Meaning?"

"Stepped on a land mine, blew off half his leg."

So that's why he's so gimpy. "I thought you could barely remember him."

Dad cups his hands around the glass and looks serious. "I remember him fine. You know, Chase, I've been thinking. Lately you've been on me about whether or not I took drugs when I was your age. I imagine that's why you brought up Chester's name in the first place."

"Actually, no." *Well, maybe…*

"Suppose I did, Chase. What does that have to do with you? If I made a mistake, does that somehow give you the green light to make the same mistake?"

"But you don't make it sound like it was a mistake, Dad. I mean, you said it was this big political statement."

"In retrospect, I think it all would have happened without drugs, too. And like I said, other things have changed since then as well."

"So, now you're saying you did take drugs?" I ask.

"Uh, not necessarily."

Jeez, Dad, make up your mind.

NICOLE

Notice anything unusual?" Alicia asks at Alex Gidden's party.

"About?"

"Who's here and who isn't."

It's not immediately obvious due to the fact that the boys are downstairs in the rec room playing Foosball.

"Brad's here, but not Little Miss Pro-Choice."

"She's probably off somewhere marching."

"At ten o'clock on a Saturday night?" Alicia shakes her head. "I don't think so. Actually, it's been days since I've seen them together. Frankly, I'm starting to think UNLIKELY COUPLE PROVES SKEPTICS RIGHT."

Funny, now that she mentions it, I realize that I haven't been paying attention. I've hardly even been *aware* of Brad lately.

"Don't let your imagination run loose," I warn her. "I'm sure things between Brad and Dulcie are just fine."

But something tells me I better check.

♛

CHASE

I'm rooting around in Alex's refrigerator when someone taps me on the shoulder. It's Nicole's foxy friend, Alicia.

"Looking for something?" She gives me a sly smile.

"Well, yeah, something to drink."

A look of surprise crosses her face. "The beer's gone?"

"No, there's plenty."

"Then what's the problem?"

"I was just looking for something, you know, non-alcoholic."

She gives me a nudge. "Oh, go on, Chase. No one's going to tell."

"It's not that," I try to explain, but who wants to sound like a dweeb?

Next thing I know, Alicia brushes tantalizingly close and pulls two cans out of the fridge. She hands one to me and pops the other open.

"Cheers," she says, with a glint in her eye.

NICOLE

After waiting forever for the Foosball game to end, I *accidentally* bump into Brad in the hall.

"Oh, Brad! I didn't see you come in." I act surprised and pretend to look around. "Where's Dulcie?"

"Don't know."

"Probably doing some kind of telephone fund-raiser. Imagine, on a Saturday night. I really admire her. She's so dedicated."

Brad shrugs his long frame, as if he isn't certain he shares my admiration. "And where's, uh…"

"Chase? In the kitchen getting something to drink."

Brad fixes me with his deep blue eyes. "Funny how things work out."

"I guess." I feel a chill. "Actually, I have a confession to make. At first I was really shocked at the thought of you and Dulcie. But the more I think about it, the more sense it makes. I mean, how can you *not* like someone like Dulcie?"

Brad blinks. "Listen, Nicole, for old times' sake, can we talk?"

Suddenly I'm feeling serious VMEs (Very Mixed Emotions). I look around for Chase, but he's nowhere in sight. Well…it can't hurt to talk, can it?

CHASE

So it's just like a fairy tale, right?" Alicia's giving me this knowing, teasing look.

"Huh?" I'm not following her too well, due to the distraction of her proximity. I'm sort of leaning against the kitchen counter and Alicia is sort of leaning toward me, just a little too close for comfort.

"I meant, you and Nicole," she says. "Childhood sweethearts who grow up and fall in love."

"Oh, uh, yeah."

She lets out a big sigh and gives me *that look*. "Too bad."

"What's too bad?"

"Well, you know." She gives me more of *that look*. "That you're taken."

"Huh?" Either she's talking in riddles or a few sips of beer has had a profound impact on my thought processes. But this is making no sense at all.

She leans closer. "I mean, who would have guessed that under that grunge look was such a studly hunk?"

Since there's no one else in the kitchen, it appears that she's talking about me. Meanwhile, she's moved closer. The scent of her perfume is in the air and she's still giving me *that look*. I'm starting to have the kind of thoughts that make women call us guys animals.

"Uh, so where's Jason?" I ask, hoping to remind her that she has a boyfriend.

"Jason who?"

"I thought..."

She moves closer. "Just tell me, are you *sure* Nicole's the one?"

If she gets any closer, we'll break the law of physics that says two objects can't occupy the same space at the same time. I can feel a buzz from head to foot. The hormones are definitely heating up. The Babe Radar is locked on an incoming object of desire. I know this isn't right, but...you know what happens when the juices start to flow.

"What are my other choices?" I ask.

"Oh, I'm sure that would be obvious if you looked around."

We're almost touching now. Suddenly the kitchen feels very warm.

NICOLE

She seemed so different," Brad's saying. We're sitting alone in the den with the door closed.

"She is different," I agree.

"She does exactly what she feels like doing. If she wants to go out, we go out. If she doesn't, it's just tough."

"You're not used to that," I observe. *Is there a guy alive who is?*

He crosses his long legs and brushes his long fingers through his dark hair. "It's not like I have a problem with her being so independent. But it's weird to be left in the dark all the time. I mean, I *never* know what she's going to do."

"Well, you know she's going to the prom with you," I point out.

"Unless she changes her mind."

My heart begins to leap, but it quickly changes its mind and keeps both feet planted firmly on the ground. We're past all that, remember? Chase and I have a scam.

"Don't be a tease, Brad," I scold.

The slight lines in Brad's high forehead deepen. "But I thought you were going with Chase."

"That's right."

I am absolutely and positively going to the prom with Chase.

Aren't I?

Funny, I look around, but all I see is you." I swallow nervously. Alicia and I are so close that I swear I can feel the heat emanating from her body. The juices are coursing through the floodgates. The noose of desire is tightening. Frustration blossoms and transmutates.

"That's because we're alone," she replies in a husky whisper.

I manage to muster my last molecule of self-control. "Then maybe it's a good time to talk about my other choices."

"Or, maybe, it's a good time not to talk at all," she purrs.

For the first time ever, Brad is actually talking to me. I mean, the *real* Brad, not the confident *GQ* Brad he pretends to be with everyone else. This is a thinking, caring Brad, a Brad with doubts and fears—a human Brad.

"It's almost the end of high school and I feel like I've been playing this role for so long that no one ever got to know the real me," he's saying. "I mean, for three years I've been the center of the basketball team and not once has anyone come up and said, 'Brad, you know what? You really suck.'"

"That's because they're your friends."

"Aren't friends supposed to be honest?" he asks. "I mean, I knew I sucked. *They* knew I sucked. How come everyone pretended I didn't?"

"You really want the truth?"

He nods.

"They had no one else to play center."

Brad studies me for a moment. "You want to know a secret, Nicole? I *hate* basketball. I really do. I hated every game, every practice. I mean, how can you like something you're lousy at?"

I'm amazed to hear this. "Why did you play all this time?"

"Because I had to. Because everyone *expected* me to.

Because…like you said, there was no one else."

"But if you *really* hated it…" I'm astonished. "I mean, all those games, all those practices."

"Nicole, with me at center, we were bad. But think what it would have been like if I wasn't there?"

He has a point. But it means he's suffered. He's been an incredible martyr.

Brad sighs. "I'll tell you one thing. I'm not playing basketball at college next year. Not even a pickup game. If anyone asks if I ever played, I'm going to say, 'Nope, never did.'"

I'm dumbstruck. Brad Selden, who seemed to have as much depth as a kiddy pool, is *deep*. He has feelings and thoughts. He's made terrible sacrifices and has borne them in stoic silence. He's…a hero!

♛

CHASE

Standing at the curb outside Alex's house, feeling sick inside, but it's not from drinking.

"Don't let it get to you," Eddie Lampel's saying. He and Alex have just escorted me out of the house.

"How am I supposed to do that?" I ask.

"She gets everyone once," Alex says. "She's just a tease."

Is Alex being honest, or just trying to make me feel better? After all, I've just suffered total humiliation. I'm still not sure how it happened. It seemed like Alicia just kept coming on to me until I said something dumb. The next thing I knew, she slapped me in the face and got really pissed. Then Eddie and Alex came in and suggested that maybe I should go outside with them.

Before we left I looked around for Nicole, but she was nowhere to be seen.

Eddie and Alex aren't mad or laughing at me or anything. Maybe Alex is telling the truth when he says Alicia gets everyone once.

But that still doesn't stop me from feeling totally and excruciatingly humiliated.

"Jeez, man, I just can't believe it," I mutter.

Eddie pats me on the back. "Welcome to the club."

"There ought to be a law against babes like that." Alex

presses one nostril closed and blows an air hanky, as if demonstrating what he thinks of Alicia.

A pair of headlights appear down the street and a car pulls up.

It stops in front of us. Eddie gets in the front and I pile into the back. I just can't believe what a fool I've been. What an *idiot*.

Hey, something smells familiar....

"Okay, guys, where to?" the driver asks.

That voice...I look up. It's Dave.

NICOLE

The door to the den opens and Angie Sunberg looks in. "Ooops, sorry, didn't mean to interrupt."

"It's okay," Brad and I reply at the same time, as if we both want her to know that *absolutely nothing* is going on.

Angie has a funny look on her face. "Have you guys been in here all this time?"

Brad and I exchange a puzzled glance.

"Why?" I ask.

"Chase was looking for you."

Brad and I share another glance.

"I think you better have a talk with Alicia," Angie says.

So what happened?" Dave asks from the front seat. We just dropped off Eddie at his house.

"I don't know. What are you talking about?"

"I got a call to come and get you guys. They said something about you and Alicia."

I slump down in the backseat. A cloud drifts overhead and starts to darken. Jeez, Dave's already heard. How long before the *entire* school hears?

And Nicole!

"Nothing happened."

"Yeah, right," Dave grumbles.

I feel bound in a straitjacket of regret. I knew I shouldn't have gotten involved with that crowd. I'm not one of *those* people. Man, *those* people are vicious.

At least Alicia is.

"So how come you're not walking tonight?" Dave asks after a while.

"Huh?"

"The other night you said you wanted to walk home."

"Oh, yeah. Not tonight," I answer absently. But maybe Eddie and Alex are telling the truth. Maybe it's just a head trip Alicia pulls on *every* new guy. In a strange way it almost makes me one of them. Like a rite of passage, an initiation. *Join the club, Chase.*

Screeech! I lurch forward and almost bang my head against the seat. Dave must have slammed the brakes. But when I look up, we're the only car on the dark street.

"Wha...? What's going on?"

Dave twists around. He's gritting his teeth. Steam is practically hissing out of his ears.

"You rot, Chase," he shouts. "You're a total lowlife, scuzzball traitor!"

"Huh?"

"I'm not good enough to talk to anymore, right?" he rants. "Now you're one of *them*. Now you're cool. You don't need your old friends because you're in with the popular crowd. Well, screw you! Get out of my car!"

"What?"

"I said, get out!" Dave shouts.

"No."

Dave glowers at me. He really looks like he's blown a fuse. "Okay, then I'll get out!"

Wham! Next thing I know, Dave gets out of his own car and slams the door.

But I was doing it for *you*," Alicia claims. She and I are alone in the den.

"*What!?*"

"I was testing him," she explains. "I wanted to see if what he felt for you was true." She puts her hand on her hip and strikes a pose. "Frankly, I think I did you a *big* favor."

"You did me a favor by hitting on the boy who's taking me to the prom?" I ask, bewildered. "What are you talking about?"

Alicia crosses her arms. "Well, it's obvious he doesn't have a clue what being faithful is about."

"How about *loyal?*" I yell at her. "Do *you* have a clue what *that's* about?"

"Grow up, Nicole." Alicia rolls her eyes. "It's not like we slept together or anything."

I could kill her.

CHASE

How long have we been friends, huh? Huh, Chase?" Dave is standing outside his car, screaming at me while I sit in the backseat. Little drops of spit are hitting the window. "I'll tell you how long. Uh…a long time. Man, we skated together, we skim boarded together. We ditched and cut and did everything together."

I just nod. My head's really starting to throb. Good thing the window's rolled up.

"And now what?" he screams. "Now I'm no good anymore. Now I get left behind because you, you dirtbag, have found the magic formula for popularity. You cut your hair and got cuffs on your pants and now you're God's gift to Time Zone High. Oh, yeah, everyone loves Chase now. Chase parties with the cool kids. Chase has a hot date for the prom. He doesn't need his old geekoid friend Dave anymore."

I roll down the window and speak as calmly as possible given the circumstances. "Dave, get back in the car."

"Don't tell me what to do!" Dave yells, and points a shaky finger at me. "Don't you *ever* tell me what to do!"

I roll the window back up. He stomps around in a circle in the middle of the dark street, clenching and unclenching his fists. I sit in the backseat of his car and tilt my head back. I've never sat in his backseat before. A small, handwritten sign is stuck to the ceiling:

IF U CN RD THS
YR SCRWD

Tap! Tap! Dave taps on the window.

I roll it down partway.

He leans in toward me, panting for breath. "Okay... just tell me one thing... just one thing... okay?"

"Sure."

He takes a deep breath and lets it out slowly. "How did you do it, Chase?"

"How'd I do what?"

"How... did... you... become... popular?"

NICOLE

The world has gone mental. My best friend puts the moves on my prom date and claims she's just testing him to see if he's being faithful. Meanwhile, the boy I wished had asked me to the prom in the first place is no longer in love with the girl he jilted me for.

I get home from the party to find all the lights on in the house. The dining room table is set for two, and it's clear from the flowers, incense, and melted candles that a romantic dinner has taken place.

With *my mother* involved?

Then I notice a man's brown crewneck sweater draped over the back of one of the chairs.

They're here!? Wait a minute! This I can't believe.

"Mom?" I look around.

No answer. Maybe they went out somewhere and he forgot his sweater…whoever *he* is.

But it's totally unlike my mother to leave the house with all the lights burning.

And why wouldn't the guy take his sweater?

"Uh, Mom? You here?"

"Yes, hon?" Her voice comes from the bedroom. I look down the hall. The bedroom door is closed.

Ohmygod!

I don't know what to say.

My mother? The woman who once said all men are a disease?

"What is it, hon?" she calls from inside the bedroom.

"Uh, nothing. I, uh, was wondering where you were."

"I'm here, hon. Why don't you go to bed? I'll see you in the morning."

Totally stunned, I stumble toward my room. My mother is in her bedroom with someone?

My mother?

CHASE

I'm lying in bed around noon, wishing it was all a bad dream.

Briiinnnggg! The phone rings. I just stare at it. It's got to be Nicole, right? She's gonna blast me, tell me to forget about the prom, tell me she never wants to see me again.

Briiinnnggg! Maybe I don't care about the prom.

But I do want to see her again.

Briiinnnggg! Guess I have to face the music. I answer.

"Chase?" It's Dulcie.

We hook up at the beach. It's a bright, sunny day, but the water's still too cold for swimming. People in bathing suits are lying on blankets. Dulcie and I walk along the water's edge with our shoes in our hands.

"So what's the story with old Stone Hands?" I ask.

"Oh, Chase," Dulcie groans, "do we have to get into that?"

"Just wondering, that's all."

"There's nothing left to wonder about."

"I thought you two were serious."

"As serious as you and Nicole?" Dulcie arches an eyebrow.

"Hey, if you could, so could I."

Dulcie smiles. "I thought so."

NICOLE

Numbness must be the body's natural defense against total VME overload. Because right now, I feel numb. Part of me wants to call Chase and scream at him. How dare he try to put the moves on my friend?

But another part wants to tell him I know that Alicia initiated it, and boys being naturally depraved, I sympathize with the temptation he faced.

But another part won't let me do that. Because our scam of the great whirlwind romance is now over. Everything was going so well. We had everyone convinced. Why did he have to fall for the *lures* of Alicia?

Meanwhile, another part of me wants to start a subtle campaign to get Brad to do what he should have done in the first place.

But yet *another* part of me is saying, "Enough already."

And still *another* part of me wants to pack a backpack and head for Europe.

Fat chance.

And finally, there's the part of me that says, "When the going gets tough, the tough go shopping."

That part wins.

♛

CHASE

It's funny how things turn out," Dulcie says as we walk along the water.

"Yeah."

"It's really silly."

"Yeah."

A wave unexpectedly races up the beach, washing over our feet.

"*Ah!*" We both let out a yell and run up to the dry, warm sand.

"I think my ankles have gone numb," she says.

"Maybe we should sit and let them warm in the sun."

We sit down and gaze out at the green waves and the sunlight sparkling on the blue water beyond them. For a while we just watch and listen to the waves crashing.

"Know what's weird?" I ask.

"What?"

"This beach has probably been here for a million years. And every day for that million years, waves have crashed on it. And a million years from now they'll still be crashing on it."

"But we won't be here," Dulcie adds.

"Right. And nothing we did or said will matter at all. I mean, I could take off my clothes and run up and down this beach nude. Or I could take a machine gun and slaughter everyone in sight. It doesn't matter. The prom, Brad, Nicole, you, me. It's like, when you come right down to it, *nothing* we do or say really matters."

"So we might as well do whatever we want?" Dulcie asks.

"I guess. I don't know. It's bizarre."

Dulcie gives me a quizzical look. "What do you want to do?"

I just shrug. Funny, but I know exactly what I want. Not that I'd tell Dulcie.

"You still want to go to the prom with Nicole, don't you?"

I just look back at her. Is *that* what this is all about?

NICOLE

Nicole?" someone says.

I'm in the swimsuit department at Nordstroms, browsing through one-pieces and trying to avoid life. Looking up from the rack, I find a vaguely familiar face. "Stacy?"

I hardly recognize her. Her face is plain and scrubbed without a hint of makeup. Her hair is flat and pulled back. She's wearing a baggy work shirt and jeans.

"My day off," she says. "My parents took Callie to the zoo. I like that."

She's talking about a black-and-gold one-piece with a price tag from hell.

"Oh, uh, just pretending." I put the suit back on the rack. "I'd have to take a loan from the bank."

"Do you really like it?" she asks.

"I won't let myself like it."

She winks. "I'll buy it for you."

"What?"

"Come on." She takes the suit and heads for the cashier.

I protest. Believe me, I do. But Stacy buys me the bathing suit because, she says, she wants to show her appreciation for the work I've done with Callie. We wind up in the food court eating frozen yogurt and talking about life.

Well, my life, that is.

"It all seems so incredibly urgent." Stacy sounds a bit wistful after I tell her the whole story of Brad, Chase, Alicia, myself, and the imminent prom.

"And someday I'll look back and I won't believe how seriously I took it, right?" I ask.

She smiles. "If you know that, then what's the problem?"

"I know it here." First I point at my head, then at my heart. "But not here. It's like I can't stop playing the game. I just want it to be perfect. I want it to be the best memory of my life."

Stacy's smile grows crooked. Reaching into her bag, she takes out a cigarette and lights it. She blows a cloud of smoke up into the air and then just gazes at it. "At least you have the brains to see it for what it really is. I never did."

"Never?"

"Not until it was too late."

Then she tells me the most amazing story.

♔

CHASE

Dulcie wants me to change my mind about taking Nicole to the prom and ask her instead. Then Brad can ask Nicole and everyone will live happily ever after.

But I won't do it.

Not to Nicole.

And not to me.

I guess I'm just tired of people using me.

Stacy had believed it all—the penultimate importance of high school social life, the prom, the feeling that nothing else mattered.

But there was life after high school, so she married her sweetheart, Dwayne. Dwayne became a roofer. He loved working outside under the sun. He could rip a roof off and hammer a new one down in a week. From April to November the money was good.

In the winter they lived on savings. Dwayne plowed driveways when it snowed.

Stacy went to junior college and studied physical therapy.

Then she had Callie.

Callie had a heart valve problem and needed three operations to correct it. Dwayne's health plan paid for some of the medical bills, but not all of them.

Then Dwayne's truck broke down.

To make extra money, Dwayne tried to do roofs straight through the winter. Through rain, sleet, or snow, windchill factor of minus twenty degrees below zero, he spent eight hours a day on roofs.

Until he slipped on an icy gutter and fell two stories.

The ground was frozen.

He broke his pelvis and had to stay in traction for eight

weeks. The health plan paid some of the bills, but not all of them. Disability insurance should have helped, but the insurance company said it was Dwayne's fault. He shouldn't have been roofing in that kind of weather. They refused to pay.

Suddenly Stacy had a broken husband and a sick child. She had to get a job. Besides all the medical and regular household bills, she had to hire someone to take care of Callie while she was out working.

When the numbers got crunched, she realized she'd have to make almost twice what Dwayne had made in his best year ever. There aren't a lot of ways for a young woman with a high school degree to make that kind of money.

But Stacy found one.

CHASE

Back home after the beach. Dad's sitting in the kitchen, gazing out into the backyard with a dreamy look on his face. On the table before him is a mug of coffee. No business papers, no spreadsheets.

"Anyone call?" I ask.

He blinks, then focuses. "Oh, yeah, Dave."

After he screamed at me last night? That's interesting. I go over to the phone and dial his number. Meanwhile, Dad just sits there.

"You okay?" I ask him while I listen to the phone ring.

"Huh? Oh, yeah."

I get Dave's answering machine and hang up, then go over to the counter and pour myself a cup of coffee. After last night, I need it.

"So how's it going?" Dad asks.

"You wouldn't believe it," I answer.

He chuckles. "I know what you mean. Actually, there's something I think we should—"

A car honks in the driveway.

"Sounds like Dave." I head through the house and out the front door. Dave sticks his head out the car window.

"Hear about Ray?" he asks.

"What now?"

"The police nailed him going the wrong way on the freeway last night."

"What!?"

"It was in the paper this morning. A freakin' miracle no one got hurt. He went about half a mile, cars skidding all over the place to get out of his way. When the cops got there, he was stopped on the shoulder, gripping the steering wheel so tight, they could hardly pry his fingers off."

"Jeez."

"They got him on reckless endangerment, driving under the influence, and about five other things."

"Driving under the influence?" It doesn't make sense. Ray never touched booze.

"Get with the program, Chase. LSD."

"Wha…?" I feel my jaw drop.

"They found a Baggie in the car with these little paper blotters in it. Paper said it has to go to the lab for analysis, but it's a common form of LSD."

"He was driving… *and tripping?*" Unbelievable!

"Puts him right up there with Branco."

Last fall, Jeff Branco became a celebrity for being the only person ever to break *into* the Fairview Home, the local girls' detention facility. His girlfriend was in there and he wanted to give her a birthday present.

"So what happens now?" I ask.

"It's survival of the fittest," Dave says with a grin.

"How's that?"

"His parents throw a fit, and he tries to survive."

NICOLE

A *stripper?*

"Hon," Stacy says, "if you don't blink sooner or later, your eyeballs are going to dry up."

I blink. "What about Dwayne?"

"Dwayne decided he liked painkillers more than roofing. Believe me, I wasn't getting naked in front of strange men six hours a night just to support his drug habit. So it was bye-bye, Dwayne."

"But Callie…"

Stacy sighs. "I know. It hurts to take her away from her daddy, but if Daddy's on drugs, it's just no good."

I can't believe this. I mean, it's like *TV.* People doing things they hate just to survive. My life is an absolute fairy tale compared to Stacy's. How could I even *care* about the prom?

"I guess you can see why I want Callie to have it better," Stacy says.

I nod. "But what about you?"

She exhales a weary stream of smoke. "A twenty-eight-year-old divorced stripper with a kid? I think Prince Charming's gonna pass."

I don't know what to say. Stacy looks at her watch. "I better get going." She starts to get up. "Callie's looking forward to seeing you Monday."

Somewhere deep inside the murky gray matter of my mind, a lightbulb pops on. "Just one last question?"

"Sure."

"Does my dad have anything to do with this?"

Stacy takes another drag on her cigarette. "Yes, Nicole, he does."

"How?" I feel myself tensing up with apprehension.

"Let's just say"—She crushes out the cigarette—"that he's one of my biggest fans."

♛

CHASE

They're home," Dave says. He and I are parked across the street from Ray's house.

"Think we should knock on the door?" I ask.

Dave gives me a look. Ray's father is this scary son-and-wife-beater type.

"On second thought, bad idea," I admit.

Dave puts the car in gear and we pull away. I know this is about Ray, but it's also about Dave and me. After the fit he threw last night, it's Dave's way of apologizing.

"I hate to say it," Dave goes, "but I have a feeling he's in for a bad time."

We drive along in silence for a moment.

"Know what I don't get?" I finally ask. "You put the guy down every chance you get. You act like you can't stand him. Then this happens and now you act like you care."

"I do care."

I give him a real questioning look.

"I know." Dave sighs. "It's weird."

Monday morning. "I thought you were in love with Chase," Alicia whispers while I put some books in my locker. The big news, of course, is about Ray Neely. But there are a few other pressing matters, such as the sudden avail-ability of Brad for the prom.

"I *am* in love with Chase," I insist. (Okay, maybe not *love*. But I really do like him. I mean, not just as a friend, either—more than that. But how much more? That I don't know.)

"Then you want to go to the prom with him."

"But who's Brad going to go with?" I ask.

"What do you care?"

How can I explain? If I switched to Brad now, every-one would assume I'd dumped Chase for him, and that wouldn't be fair to Chase. But if I don't switch to Brad, some other girl will. And if Brad goes to the prom with anyone else, I'll die! But I like Chase. I *want* to go to the prom with him.

"It's very, very complicated," I try to explain.

"Funny, it seems very *un*complicated to me," Alicia responds.

"*Alllleeeeeeessssshhhhhhaaaaa!*" The scream reverberates down the crowded hallway. Alicia and I spin around just in time to see Mr. Rope's hand clamp down on Karl Lukowsky's shoulder.

"Gotcha!" Mr. Rope cries with delight as he yanks Karl backward toward the office.

"*I looooovvve you!*" Karl screams as he's dragged away.

Alicia rolls her eyes. "SCREAMING STALKER SEES SUSPENSION."

♕

CHASE

By lunchtime they're calling him "Wrong Way" Ray.

"All of a sudden he's an overnight sensation," Dave grumbles as we slide our trays along the lunch line. "Everybody's acting like they're his oldest and dearest friend. Maybe tonight *I'll* drive the wrong way on the freeway."

"It's not in your character." I pick out a brownie.

"Maybe not, but it could make me *popular* like you." Pure resentment.

"The jocks won't want you to drive them anymore."

We pay for lunch and find a table. But Dave doesn't eat. He just sits with his chin resting in his hand.

"What is it?" I ask.

"You're right," he says glumly. "I have only one function in life—driving the drunk jocks around. I'm Designated Dave, and that's all I'll ever be."

His shoulders slump as he starts to slide down the slippery slope of self-pity.

"Then stop driving them," I tell him.

"What?" Dave looks astonished. "Are you serious?"

"Sure. If you don't want them to use you, then stop."

"I can't."

"Why not?" I ask.

"Because then what would I do?"

At our weekly PPC meeting, everyone's talking about Ray.

"At least what Jeff Branco did was romantic," Chloe says. "Ray was just plain dumb."

"He deserves it," Sandy Kimmel states flatly. "I hate the way he gets high in school. Like he's flaunting it. And he's so weird-looking."

"Don't you think that's a little harsh?" I ask.

Sandy looks down her nose at me. "No."

"People who take drugs have problems," I point out.

"So *what else* is new?" Alicia gives me a puzzled "that's-totally-obvious" look.

"I mean, they're in pain," I try to explain.

"We're not talking about painkillers," Sandy says. "Ray was on LSD."

"It's the same thing," I go. "Maybe he wasn't in *physical* pain, but the very fact that he was getting stoned a lot meant that he must have been in emotional pain."

The rest of the prom committee exchanges dubious glances.

"Look, Nicole," Sandy says. "*All* of us feel some emotional pain now and then, but we don't go around stoned all day long because of it."

"Well, then maybe we're better equipped to deal with the pain than he was," I reply. "Or maybe Ray's pain was a lot greater than we ever suspected."

A moment of silence descends on our little circle of desks.

"*Ahem.*" Chloe clears her throat, and opens a notebook. "I'd just like to report on the current state of ticket sales."

While Chloe reads off the numbers, I wonder why I came to Ray's defense. Why do I even care?

I ran into Ray's brother," Dave says the next morning. We're sitting in his car in the parking lot, waiting for school to start.

"And?"

"They put him in rehab."

"That's it?"

"No. He still has to go to court. His lawyer figures he'll get a suspended sentence, probation, and no driver's license until he turns twenty-one."

"When does he come back to school?"

"After rehab, I guess."

"Amazing."

Someone taps on the window. It's Alicia. "Could I speak to you for a moment?"

Naturally, I'm just slightly wary after what she did to me at the party. "Drop dead, skank."

"Look, Chase, I'm sorry about the party. I really didn't mean to mislead you."

"Get lost."

"I know you must be really angry, but I already told Nicole it wasn't your fault."

I eye her suspiciously.

"This is really important, Chase."

"Yeah, right." Like I'd believe anything she'd say.

"It's about Nicole."

I glance over at Dave, who's been listening.

"Can't hurt to hear her out," he says with a shrug.

I get out of the car. Alicia moves a few cars over so Dave won't hear. Then she crosses her arms. "Do you know what's going on with Nicole?"

"No."

"She's got a problem."

"What kind of problem?"

Alicia lets out a big sigh, as if this is going to be really difficult for her to talk about. "Well, you know how much she likes you and wants to go to the prom with you."

I just nod.

"But she's got a certain position in our, er, sphere that she has to occupy."

Did she just say *sphere?*

"Like what?" I ask.

"Well, like with the prom coming up and Brad having no one to go with…"

"So?"

Alicia doesn't answer. She just gives me this look that says, "Don't you get it?"

And I stare at her in disbelief. Because I do get it. It's *those* people again, and those people are vicious. I've never been one and I'll never be one. I just don't *care* that much.

But Nicole. I can't believe she'd do this….

And at the same time I can.

"Does Nicole know you're talking to me about this?" I ask.

Alicia shakes her head. "No, but being her friend, I'm just trying to help."

NICOLE

can't believe you. *I just can't believe you!*"

"Please stop screaming." I've never seen Chase so livid. Luckily we're in the park after school and no one's around.

Chase's face is red. "After everything I did for you!"

"For me?" I have to laugh.

"Yeah, for *you!* I changed my hair, I changed my clothes. I agreed to go to the stupid prom. I sat around at parties talking about basketball players I'd never even heard of. You think I *liked* that?"

"Oh, poor Chase." I pretend to pout. "I bet it was really difficult to become popular. I bet you hated every second of it."

Chase glares at me. He's panting from all the yelling.

"Anyway, I don't understand what you're so mad about," I tell him. "No one said I was going to go to the prom with Brad."

"Just the idea that you'd even *consider* it," Chase seethes.

"Don't you ever consider things?" I ask. "I mean, it's human nature."

"Yeah," Chase mutters. "It's human nature to screw over your close friend just so you can go to a stupid prom with a *GQ* dork and impress everyone."

"You're being mean, Chase," I warn him.

Chase glares at me. "Oh, yeah? Well, you're a lowlife, manipulative slime."

That's where the conversation ends. I don't have to take that from anyone.

"Chase Hammond is the most insensitive, ungrateful, thick-skulled idiot I've ever had the displeasure to know!" I shout as I slam through the front door.

Mom pops out of the kitchen with a concerned look on her face. "Hon—"

"I can't believe I even *considered* going to the prom with that jerk!" I stomp past Mom and into the kitchen where…Rob, Chase's dad, is sitting. "Oh, uh, hi, Mr. Hammond. I didn't know you were here."

Rob is rising out of his chair. "I, er, think I better go."

Talk about total humiliation. I can feel my face burn. It must be beet-red with embarrassment. Rob leaves. Mom gives me the hairy eyeball and then follows him to the door.

"Wait, Rob!"

They don't understand. They *can't* understand.

Briiinnnggg! It's the phone. I grab it. "Hello?"

"It's me." Alicia.

"I've had it with Chase," I tell her. "He just doesn't have a clue. It's hopeless. I can't believe I wasted my time on him. I—"

"Bet you're wondering why I called," Alicia says.

"Oh, sorry. I got carried away."

"You'll never guess who just called me."

"Who?"

"Brad."

"Brad?" I'm so out of it. "Why?"

"Well…to ask me to the prom."

Prom night.

A month since Nicole and I "broke up."

A couple of hours ago a long white limo pulled up in front of her house. I watched from the living room window as her date jumped out and went to get her. I knew they were going to the pre-prom party at Chloe's house. I was invited, too, but I didn't feel like going.

Now Dad's giving me and Mrs. Maris a ride to school. Dad's got his video recorder and Mrs. Maris is armed with a camera so that they can be among the hundreds of parents recording the Grand March for their future Grand Children.

We actually have to park on the street outside school. I've never seen the parking lot so jammed with cars and limos. Dad and Mrs. Maris are supposed to go into the cafeteria where the Grand March will be held. I have to go through the main doors to the lobby, where the participants will all get in line.

We get out of the car. Dad straightens my bow tie.

"You sure you want to do this?" he asks.

"Yeah, no sweat."

He smiles. "Okay, sport. Knock 'em dead."

♔

NICOLE

I think it's really important to help people through the rough times in their lives. That's why I decided to go to the prom with Ray. He's out of rehab now and is a completely different person than before. He even got a haircut. I couldn't have done a better makeover on him myself (that's a joke).

Besides, on the basis of his new-found notoriety alone, we're definitely in the Top Twelve.

At Chloe's pre-prom party, Alicia clings to Brad, and beams. Would you believe I haven't said a word to her since she told me he asked her to the prom? At first I was so angry, I would have gladly tied her to an exploding cow.

But after a while I started to miss her.

Of course, I couldn't say so because of the pride thing. But at the party she comes over.

"Do you still hate me?" she asks.

"Yes." But I smile because it's not entirely true.

She smiles back. "I'm leaving for France tomorrow night."

"What about graduation?"

"They can fax my diploma. Or keep it for all I care."

So that's it. "Well, I guess you won."

Alicia's smile fades. "That's really not what it's about, Nicole."

Part of me knows she's right. Part of me isn't so sure.

"Look around," she says.

I scope the crowd of tuxedoed boys and gowned girls standing around Chloe's pool, holding drinks and munching on hors d'oeuvres. Kids I'd known forever. It's funny how grown up they look.

"High school's over," Alicia goes. "Half of them are going away to college. The rest will probably get jobs. It won't matter anymore who's popular and who's not."

Everything I cared so much about . . .

"I never understood why it was so important to you." It's as if she can read my mind. "I guess maybe because I moved around so much growing up, I learned early that it doesn't matter what other people think of you. What matters is what you think of yourself. Everyone you know changes sooner or later. You're the one person you really have to learn to live with."

Brad comes up beside her and hands her a glass. He smiles at me. "Hey, Nicole."

He looks great in his tux, and Alicia looks fabulous, albeit slightly slutty, in her slinky gown.

"You two look totally smashing together," I tell them. And I wouldn't mind "smashing" them both.

We stand there with frozen smiles for a moment.

"You know," Brad finally says, "it's too bad you're only allowed to take one date to the prom. I would have liked to take you both."

"Oh, you're just saying that." I pooh-pooh it.

Brad fixes me with those steely blue eyes. "No, Nicole, I really mean it."

Yes, it's funny how things turn out.

♔

CHASE

I go in the main doors. Everyone's milling around in their tuxes and gowns, waiting for the Grand March to begin.

Mr. Rope is standing near the entrance to the cafeteria. "All right, everybody!" he's yelling. "Time to get in line. You'll go in one couple at a time. Get in line, everybody!"

But the crowd continues to mill around like a big herd of sheep that can't decide what direction to take.

"Chase?"

I turn and find Dave and Dulcie giving me a surprised look. Dulcie got him to ask her to the prom the day after she and I went to the beach.

"What are you doing here?" Dave asks.

"What's it look like?" I ask.

"Who's your date?" asks Dulcie.

"Don't have one."

We're all outside the cafeteria, waiting for the Grand March to begin. Ray has just spent the last twenty minutes explaining popularity to me in terms of Darwinism and natural selection.

"You're saying it's all programmed into our genes?" I ask. "It's human nature?"

"That's it," Ray says. "You almost can't help yourself. Even when you think you know better."

I'm fascinated. According to Ray, I'm not abnormal for caring so much. For instance, at this moment I'm acutely aware of the subtle maneuvering as couples prepare for the Grand March. The most popular couples are gravitating toward the back of the crowd, or at least away from the entrance to the cafeteria. Even though Alicia is probably right that it won't mean anything much longer, we can't help ourselves.

It's in our genes.

"Nicole?"

It's the last voice I'd expect to hear. "Dad! What are you doing here?"

My father has come with his camera. He's wearing a new, shorter, darker rug on his head. "I had to see you on your prom night. May I say that you look wonderful." He's beaming with pride.

"But what about Mom? You're not supposed to—"

"Shhh…" He presses his finger to his lips. "She doesn't have to know."

"Well, this is Ray. Ray, this is my dad." I introduce them.

"Hey, Mr. Maris." Ray shakes his hand.

"Thank you for taking my daughter to the prom," Dad says. "You've made her very happy."

"No sweat, man."

Dad motions us together. "Now how about a picture?"

Ray and I stand together, and Dad's camera flashes.

"Thank you." He looks so proud and happy.

I ask Ray if he'd mind giving us a moment in private. Dad and I walk over to the windows, away from the crowd.

"He seems like a nice boy," Dad says.

"He is, Dad. Now listen, there's something I want to tell you. About a month ago I ran into Stacy. She told me about…uh, you and her."

Dad nods. "I know."

"You're not upset?" I ask.

"Actually, I'm relieved. You're a big girl now."

"Dad, I still don't get it."

"I understand. It's not what you'd expect."

"That's putting it mildly. I mean, you don't even know her."

"Well, that's not true. I see her often. Sometimes we even talk."

"Where?"

"The Platinum Paradise."

"But, I mean, that's her *job*."

"I know."

A lightbulb flashes on in my head, then explodes. "*That's* why you wanted me to tutor Callie?"

"No. Callie needed help and you needed a job. But I won't tell Stacy you told me anything."

I just stare at him in disbelief. "Dad, of all the women…"

"I know, hon." He nods. "Believe me, I was as surprised as you."

"But how?"

"I love her, Nicky. That's all that matters to me right now."

"But you're…you're sixteen years older than her."

He looks surprised. "She's twenty-eight?"

"You didn't know?"

"Well, I guessed she was around that. Tell me, hon, do you know if there's, er, *anyone special* in her life?"

"No one besides Callie."

"Good." He self-consciously touches his new toupee.

"It's *not* good, Dad, it's —"

Dad presses his finger against his lip. "I don't want you to get upset. This is your prom and I want you to enjoy it. Don't worry about me. I know what I'm doing."

"But why?"

"Love and hope, hon. The two most powerful forces in life. Once you understand that, little else matters."

♛

CHASE

The Grand March has started. The music begins, and the first couple steps in through the cafeteria doors. The crowd inside starts to clap and cheer.

I duck into the boys' room. The place is packed with guys sprucing up in front of the mirrors before the big event. I'm trying to work my way in when I come face-to-face with Dave.

"Hey, Chase."

"Hey, Dave."

We start to pass each other, then Dave grabs my arm. "You're not mad, are you?"

"What about?"

"Dulcie and me."

"Why should I be?"

"Well, she told me about you and her," he says.

"She did?"

"Yeah, and well, I just hope you understand why she said no."

What's he talking about? "Said no about what?"

"About going to the prom with you. It's just that, well, to tell you the truth, she wanted to go with someone she felt comfortable with, and since she hardly knows you…"

"*That's* what she told you?"

Dave looks puzzled. "Yeah. Why?"

That total liar! Talk about playing games!

"Nothing." I just shake my head and smile.

"Is there something else?" Dave asks.

"No, Dave, really. Go have a good time."

The boys' room empties out as guys hurry back to their dates and get in line for the Grand March. Pretty soon it's empty except for the sinks, the urinals, the stalls, and me in my tuxedo. Forty years' worth of guys have passed through this bathroom on prom night. Probably another forty years' worth still to go. Kids who haven't even been born yet. Some guys who've probably already died.

Life goes on.

I'm just about to leave the bathroom when the door swings open and Chester Potts gimps in, pushing his bucket and mop. He stops and scowls when he sees me. "Yo, Chase, better get goin' or you'll miss the Grand March."

I start past him, then stop. "Hey, Chester?"

"Say what?"

"You remember a guy in high school named Rob Hammond?"

"Rob Hammond...Rob Ham————" A big gap-toothed smile appears on his face. "You mean *Robbie* Hammond? Oh, sure, man. I knew him good."

"You guys hung together?"

"Better believe it, man. Robbie and I did some serious groovin'. The Dead would come around and he and I would be there every night, man, *every* night. Homework, school ...forget it. Only thing that mattered was goin' to see the Dead and gettin'...uh...uh...why'd you want to know about Robbie?"

"No particular reason." I just smile. Maybe Dad's right. It doesn't matter what your parents did. What matters is what you do.

NICOLE

Ray and I make the Top Twelve. As we stroll down the red-carpeted promenade, people clap and cheer. Mom's camera is flashing, and, next to her, Mr. Hammond's video camera captures Ray and me for posterity. A lot of people clap for Ray. I think they're glad to see him back in one piece in time to graduate.

Then we join the crowd to cheer as the rest of the couples come down the promenade...Chloe and her boyfriend, Kyle and his girlfriend, Eddie and Bo (I mean Dee)...and then, finally, Alicia and Brad. And even though Alicia is walking where I could have been walking, I cheer for her.

And frankly, I really don't think all that time and energy I spent being concerned with the *P*-word was a waste. Sometimes you have to experience something to understand it and grow. You can't just stand on the edge and watch.

Life is experience.

There's no such thing as wasting time.

You learn from everything you do.

Alicia and Brad finish their promenade. The music ends and all the families start packing up their cameras.

Suddenly there's a gasp and a hush.

Everyone turns toward the entrance to the cafeteria.

Where Chase is standing on the red carpet.

Alone.

CHASE

They're totally shocked. I mean, here I am, the last person down the promenade, walking alone.

For a moment there's absolute silence.

The music's stopped. I can hear the pad of my footsteps on the long red carpet. Hundreds of eyes are staring at me.

A few months ago, being in this position, feeling all their eyes on me, I couldn't have taken it.

Maybe that's why I always preferred being on the outside, acting like I didn't care. It felt safer out there. But it was only an act.

Because I did care.

Now it feels okay.

And the weird thing is, I only have Nicole to thank for it.

NICOLE

He's walking down the red carpet, tall and good-looking. And even though he's wearing a tux like the rest of the boys, I know he's different.

And the crowd starts to whisper.

Then the whispers become chuckles.

And then they start to clap and cheer.

And the prom music starts again.

And this big emotional bubble starts to rise up inside me. I'm proud of him.

And envious.

And jealous.

And mostly I just want to be with him.

Tomorrow, and the day after.

And the day after that.

Ray has to leave before midnight because of his suspended sentence and probation curfew.

So then Nicole and I get together.

It's this amazing, magical kind of thing. Like with all the pressure off and all the pretense and phoniness gone...

We're together at all the after-prom parties, and at the beach the next day. Suddenly it's pretty clear that whatever we're feeling, it's real.

And finally we go home, tired and sunburned and totally partied out. I walk Nicole up the path to her house and we stop at the front door and face each other.

"Well, uh, it's been fun." I sort of grin, feeling fuzzy and dull-witted from lack of sleep.

"It's been more than fun, Chase." Nicole gazes up at me with this gooey look in her eyes.

"Yeah, funny how things work out."

"I'm glad, aren't you?"

"Oh, yeah."

"See you tomorrow?" she asks.

"Definitely."

And we're just about to kiss when the door swings open, and Mrs. Maris is standing there.

"You're back!" she gasps. "How was it?"

Nicole and I glance at each other a little nervously because we haven't quite figured out how to break the news to our parents.

"It was great, Mom." Nicole winks at me and then starts into the house.

"Come in, Chase," Mrs. Maris says.

"Oh, uh, no thanks," I tell her. "I'm really dragging. Think I'll just go home and sleep."

"Just come in for a moment." She actually takes my arm and leads me in. "There's something we want to tell you."

We? What's she talking about? *Who is we?*

Inside, Dad steps out of the kitchen.

What's he doing here?

Mrs. Maris steps over to him and they slide their arms around each other's waist.

"Kids," Dad says, "there's something we want to tell you."

"It shouldn't come as a surprise," Mrs. Maris adds.

"Mom, what're you talking about?" Nicole gasps.

Dad and Mrs. Maris give each other this warm, happy, cuddly look.

"Nicole," Dad says, "your mom and I have decided to live together."

"So now you really will be like brother and sister," her mom says.

Nicole and I just stare at each other.

Huh?